PEN PALS: BOOK NINE

STOLEN PEN PALS

by Sharon Dennis Wyeth

A YEARLING BOOK

Published by
Dell Publishing
a division of
Bantam Doubleday Dell Publishing Group, Inc.
666 Fifth Avenue
New York, New York 10103

ISBN: 0-440-40342-1
Published by arrangement with Parachute Press, Inc.
Printed in the United States of America
May 1990
10 9 8 7 6 5 4 3 2 1
OPM

For Harriet Weitzner

CHAPTER 1

Lisa McGreevy finished a cartoon sketch of her suitemate Amy Ho on a piece of notebook paper, then turned back to her Latin book with a sigh. "I really want to do well on the test tomorrow, but I just can't concentrate," she complained.

"You need something to eat," Amy suggested, springing up from the sitting-room floor where she had been doing some kneebends.

"So do I!" Shanon Davis chimed in. She looked hungrily over the top of the newspaper she'd been reading. It was published by the nearby boys' school—Ardsley Academy.

"I'm starving," added Palmer Durand, flipping her wavy blond hair out of her eyes. "Let's go down to the dining room now. If we hurry, we'll be first in line."

The four girls roomed together at Alma Stephens School for Girls just outside the quiet New Hampshire town of Brighton. Since being assigned to Suite 3-D in Fox Hall, the four third-formers, as freshmen at Alma were called, had become close friends.

1

"I think that's a great idea," Lisa said, starting to stand up, too. "Why don't we—"

Just then Shanon let out a loud yip. "Oh, wow! Look at this!" She held up a page of advertisements.

The bottom half was taken up with a dozen or so of the usual For Sale items. But at the top was a single ad featuring a black and white photograph of four girls. Underneath was a boldly printed caption:

ATTENTION—BOYS WANTED!

WE'RE FOUR PREPETTES IN SEARCH OF PEN PALS FROM ARDSLEY ACADEMY. IF YOU ARE INTERESTED, WRITE TO "THE SISTERS" AT BRIER HALL.

"I don't believe it!" Amy gasped.

"That's almost an exact copy of *our* advertisement last September!" Lisa said indignantly. "Those copycats!"

"Let *me* see!" Palmer snatched the paper out of Shanon's hands. "I wonder who took their photo. It's not bad at all. They certainly do look like prepettes," she smirked, "complete with cashmere sweaters and pearls."

Lisa looked over her shoulder and groaned. "What are you smiling about, Palmer?" she said. "Those girls are totally gorgeous."

"They aren't *that* great-looking," Palmer argued. "Well, maybe they're just a little attractive, in a fake sort of way. But they're certainly no competition for me—I mean, for us," she corrected loyally.

"I can't believe this," Amy said, taking the paper from

Palmer. "Advertising for pen pals at Ardsley was our idea."

"I just had a terrible thought," Shanon murmured.

"What?" the others chorused.

"Well, what if our pen pals . . . you know. . . ." She looked helplessly at her friends, but they just stared back blankly, waiting for her explanation. "What if *they*—Rob, John, Mars, and Sam—decide to dump *us* for *them*?" she went on.

"That's ridiculous!" Palmer huffed. "The boys would never do that."

Amy looked doubtfully at the photo. "I don't know. These girls are awfully sophisticated-looking, not to mention cute."

"In a fake sort of way," Palmer repeated, squinting at the photo. "I bet those aren't even real pearls. Listen." She took the paper back and tossed it on the pink loveseat. "I wouldn't even give it a thought if they weren't Brier girls. But that type can be so sneaky."

In fact, the two schools, Alma Stephens and Brier Hall, had been arch rivals for years. Competing for the girls' soccer championship was one thing, Amy thought, but competing for boys was something else!

"However," Palmer continued, "when it comes down to it, they're no match for us."

"That's right," Lisa said. "There's nothing to worry about. Our pen pals will probably see the ad and laugh themselves silly. Why write to the Sisters when they can write to the Foxes of the Third Dimension? The Unknowns like *us*!" she went on, referring to the code name the girls in Suite 3-D had used when they first placed *their* ad in

3

the Ardsley paper—and the name the boys had used to answer it.

The other Foxes agreed. And after they'd all brushed their hair and touched up the light makeup that was all Miss Pryn, the strict headmistress, would allow, they headed off for dinner.

As they hurried down the hallway, they passed clusters of girls chattering excitedly. The main topic of conversation seemed to be Visitor's Day, only a few weeks away. Some of the older students had invited their boyfriends.

Lisa thought it would be nice to have a real boyfriend, someday. But for now she had her pen pal, Rob Williams, and he was pretty special.

The end of the hallway near the stairs was empty, and in the sudden silence, Lisa heard a strange sound. "Wait!" she said suddenly, coming to a standstill in front of a closed door. "What's that?"

"What's what?" Palmer said impatiently.

"Shhh!" hissed Amy, dramatically narrowing her dark brown eyes. "I heard something, too."

Then they all heard it: a muffled noise coming from behind Kate Majors's door.

"The light's on," Lisa pointed out. "You can see it through the crack. Kate must still be in there."

"It sounds like someone's crying," whispered Shanon, her pretty, warm hazel eyes wide with concern. Turning to Palmer, who was the group's authority on etiquette, she asked, "Do you think we should knock to see if she's okay? We don't want to embarrass her."

Palmer considered the problem for a moment. "We can

knock, but don't let on that anything's wrong. We'll just say we're inviting her to come to dinner with us."

The other two girls nodded in agreement, and Shanon rapped lightly on the door. There was no answer, but the snuffling noises stopped.

"Try again," Lisa said, nudging her roommate.

Shanon rapped a second time, then called out softly, "Kate, do you want to go down to dinner with us?"

After a minute, the door slowly swung open. Kate Majors stood in the space, her eyes red and teary behind her thick glasses. She smiled weakly. "Guess I might as well."

"Oh, Kate, what's wro—"

Palmer silenced Shanon with a warning look. "If we hurry," she interrupted smoothly, "we'll be first in line and get the best table. Come on."

Kate hesitated, looking at each of their faces with a puzzled expression. Shanon flushed as she realized how strange the invitation must sound. It wasn't often that the Foxes asked their dorm monitor to join them for dinner—in fact, she wasn't sure they'd ever made a point of doing it before. But Kate just shrugged and closed the door behind her, following them down the stairs.

The girls made it through the cafeteria line and to their favorite table without asking Kate why she'd been crying, and without Kate volunteering the information. The four Foxes ate in silence. But Kate didn't take a single bite of her dinner, not even the delicious warm bread, and that wasn't like her at all.

Shanon played with a row of green peas on her fork. Of all the Foxes, she was the closest to Kate—they'd been

5

working together on the Alma *Ledger* all year—and she hated to see her friend so upset.

"You don't seem very hungry, Kate," she blurted out at last.

"I guess I'm not," Kate said, lowering her eyes.

Shanon patted Kate's back gently. "Look, if something's wrong, Kate, you can tell us. Maybe talking about it will help."

"I d-d-doubt that," Kate stammered, then let out a low groan. "Oh, this is so-o-o humiliating! I just can't talk about it."

Palmer's ears perked up. "Humiliating?" She loved gossip—the juicier, the better. "What's going on, Kate? You can tell us. Who knows, maybe we can help."

"Come on, Kate," Lisa coaxed. "Even if we can't help, we can keep a secret. And you'll probably feel better just talking about it."

Kate took a deep breath and looked around the table at the four girls. "It's Reggie!" she finally said.

"Reggie!" Lisa jumped to her feet. Reggie McGreevy was Lisa's older brother. He attended Ardsley Academy. And ever since he and Kate had met at the Alma-Ardsley Halloween Mixer, they'd become something of an item.

"What's wrong with him?" Lisa cried. "What happened?"

"I don't know," Kate wailed, throwing up her hands in dismay. "He just stopped writing to me."

"He stopped writing? That's *all*?" Reassured that nothing serious had happened to her brother, Lisa sat down again.

"Well, how would *you* feel if Rob stopped writing to you?" Kate demanded.

"He wouldn't stop, ever," Lisa said firmly. "We're steady pen pals. Just like Shanon and Mars, and Amy and John—"

"And me and Sam," Palmer added proudly.

"I don't think you should worry," Lisa told Kate, digging into her Yorkshire pudding with renewed appetite. "He's probably just studying for a test or something. You know how serious he gets about stuff like that. Anyway, he was never much of a letter writer."

"He was with me," Kate objected mournfully. "And it's been *two weeks* since his last letter!"

"I'm sure one will come soon," Shanon predicted sympathetically. "Cheer up."

"Eat," Amy urged, pushing her empty dinner plate away and reaching for dessert. "This blueberry pie looks great!"

"Now wait just a minute," Palmer interrupted. "There's something we're forgetting."

"What's that?" Amy asked, looking up from her pie.

"That advertisement in the Ardsley *Lion*. Maybe Reggie has found another pen pal—someone with a phony smile and phony pearls?"

Lisa dropped her fork. "Oh, gosh! I don't think he'd do anything like that—dump Kate for a Brier girl!"

"Think again, Lisa!" Palmer said coolly. "You saw that photograph in the paper. Those girls were really cute!" She flashed a guilty look at Kate, who looked even plainer than usual with her pale face and red-rimmed eyes. "Sorry, Kate."

"It's okay," Kate said, her cheeks flushing. She pushed her glasses back up the bridge of her nose. "I know I'm not gorgeous or anything. But I thought Reggie and I had a lot in common. I really like him. Now I'm just so embarrassed about this whole thing." And with that, she stood up and ran out of the dining room.

Shanon looked at Amy. "This is terrible. Imagine getting dumped by your pen pal."

"I wouldn't stand for it," Palmer said haughtily. "I'd tell Sam off if he ever did that to me. But," she added quickly, "of course, he wouldn't."

Lisa shook her head. "I'm beginning to wonder. I mean, if it could happen to Kate, why not us?"

"Oh, no!" Amy cried, jumping up from her chair.

"What's wrong?" the other three girls asked.

"I just thought of something. Something really awful."

"What is it?" Shanon asked, looking alarmed.

"Come on!" cried Amy. "There's something I have to show you all."

Although Lisa and Shanon hadn't finished their dessert, they dumped their trays and hurried off after Palmer and Amy.

Once they were back inside Suite 3-D, Amy fished out an old copy of the Ardsley literary magazine.

"Remember that poem John had published in the lit. mag?" she asked.

"Sure," Lisa said. "That was really cool."

"Well, I was thinking about it just a moment ago. And there's something very strange about it."

Palmer raised one eyebrow and smiled archly. "Most of John's poems are pretty strange, if you ask me."

"Don't be mean, Palmer," Amy said. "I'm talking about his acrostic."

"His acrostic?" Palmer echoed vaguely.

"You know," Amy said impatiently. "It's a kind of poem

8

where the beginning letters of each line spell out a secret word. John writes a lot of them."

"That's right," Lisa chimed in. "I think they're kind of neat."

"Not so neat when you get the message." Amy held up the poem so they could all read it again.

Feeling proud
Amy—the afternoon you came to me, wearing
Red and that smile and those black jeans
Even though I was shaking in my boots
Wielding power—I was the star poet that day!
Early sunrise is nothing
Limp, cloudless weather compared to your
Liveliness!

"What's so strange about the acrostic?" Lisa said thoughtfully.

Palmer rolled her big blue eyes. "That's no secret. F-A-R-E-W-E-L-L. Get it? Farewell. I can't believe you didn't figure it out right away!"

Lisa turned from Palmer to Amy. "But what does it mean? It sounds like he's saying good-bye or something."

"I know," Amy said grimly. "Maybe John was saying good-bye . . . to *me*!"

Shanon wet her lips nervously. "Oh, this is terrible. It's all beginning to fit together. First Reggie stops writing to Kate. Then John sends a secret farewell message to Amy. Soon the others will stop writing, too, because they'd rather have those Brier girls for pen pals. They—"

"Don't you think you're jumping to conclusions?"

9

Palmer broke in. "I mean, let's not get hysterical about this!"

Shanon looked at Palmer, then at Amy and Lisa for reassurance. But suddenly Suite 3-D at Fox Hall was very quiet.

CHAPTER 2

Lisa couldn't sleep that night. When she went to take her Latin test in Thurber Hall the next morning, her eyes burned and her head ached miserably. After struggling through the questions as best she could, she handed the test in with a sigh.

She met Shanon on the sidewalk outside the building. The day was sunny, with a cool breeze just right for the long, rainbow-striped sweater she was wearing.

"Do you think Reggie would really just drop Kate?" Shanon asked after they'd walked a little way.

Lisa had always thought she and her brother were pretty close, but now she wasn't so sure.

"I don't know," she admitted. "He's normally so bashful around girls. In fact, it took a lot of nerve for him to start writing to Kate in the first place. I can't really imagine him going through all that again with someone new."

"So you think he'll keep writing to Kate?" Shanon prodded.

Lisa stopped in the middle of the quad and adjusted the orange bow in her dark brown hair. "I certainly hope so," she said vehemently.

Shanon gave her roommate a puzzled look. Kate wasn't the most popular girl in Fox Hall, and for a while Lisa had been her harshest critic. The two girls were friendly enough now, Shanon thought, but that wasn't the same thing as being *friends*.

"Oh, Kate's all right," Lisa said, as if she could read Shanon's mind. "And I'd hate to think of Reggie intentionally doing anything to hurt her feelings. Besides, dropping *any* Alma girl for a Brier girl would definitely be a low blow."

"So, do you think he'll keep writing to Kate?" Shanon repeated.

"We'll find out soon enough," Lisa said. "I'm going to write him a letter today." Lisa glanced at her watch. "In fact, I have a free period now. I could write it and drop it in the mail at Booth Hall before History."

Shanon's eyes lit with excitement. "Can I read it?"

"Sure," Lisa said agreeably. "In fact, you can help. You're the writer in the suite. You can give me ideas so it won't sound too nosey."

The girls found a wooden bench out of the wind and sat down. Lisa opened a notebook on her knees, took a ballpoint out of her purse, and started writing.

Dear Reggie,

How are you doing? I'm fine. I was just thinking how long it's been since I wrote to you. A lot is happening here at

12

Alma, and I figured you might be interested in hearing about my life—you know, the same way I'm always interested in hearing about anything new in your life.

"Oh, that's really good," Shanon approved. "Maybe you should say something more about brothers and sisters needing to keep in touch. That way he'll feel he has to tell you something really personal about himself."

"And as far as Reggie's concerned, there's nothing more personal than girls!" Lisa giggled, turning back to her letter.

I really, really believe brothers and sisters should stay close. Families are so important. Anyway—I thought you'd like to know that we have a Visitor's Day coming up next month. It would be great if you could come by then.

All the Foxes are going to the mall next weekend. We're all going to get passes and ride there on our bikes. Palmer wants to buy a new spring outfit (as if she needs any more clothes), Shanon wants to check out the bookstore, and Amy has been saving up for a new rock tape. I'm thinking of taking up knitting, so maybe I'll get some yarn and try it out. I think it would be neat to be able to make my own sweaters. Remember how Mom used to knock them out in just a couple weeks? I could create my own designs and make one for each of my suitemates! If you're good, maybe I'll even make one for you.

Well, now it's your turn to write. I want to know everything that's happening in your life, dear brother. Like, how are you and Kate doing with your own letters? She

13

writes such nice, intelligent letters, don't you think?
  Anyway, write soon.

Your loving sister,
Lisa

P.S. Remember how worried I was about my Latin paper?
Well, I got a B on it! I hope I did as well on the quiz today.
P.P.S. By the way, did you see that tacky ad in the Ardsley
Lion, *the one from the four Brier girls?*

"I don't know," Shanon said, shaking her head. "Maybe that's laying it on a little thick. You sound so sweet and angelic. He might get suspicious."

"You're right," Lisa agreed after rereading her letter. "I'll take off the 'dear brother.'"

"And the 'loving sister' too," Shanon advised. "Just 'Love, Lisa' will do. You don't want to sound too obvious."

CHAPTER 3

Dear Lisa,

    I certainly was surprised to get your letter. I don't get many from you.

    As usual, your suitemates sound like real dweebs. What's the big deal about going to the mall?

    I'm glad to hear about your B in Latin, though. Knowing how hard it is for you, I figure you must really be working at it. As for me, I expect to get all A's again, as usual.

    But I don't believe you wrote to me to check up on my grades. Lisa, why do you want to know about me and Kate? Never mind, I think I can guess. Kate must have put you up to writing that letter, to nag me about writing to her.

    Well, I don't appreciate your butting in like this. Yes, I did stop writing to Kate. And maybe I should have written her to explain things instead of just stopping—but I didn't know what to say. I mean, Kate is a nice girl, and she's very smart. But she's not exactly . . . well, you know.

    Anyway, there's this girl at Brier Hall. Her name is Cindy, and she's really pretty. And NO she isn't one of those girls in the ad. (Your hints are pretty obvious, Lisa.) I met her in Brighton a couple of weeks ago and we've been writing since then. Actually, I do more writing than she does. She doesn't like to write letters much.

If it will make you feel better, I promise to write Kate soon and tell her why I can't keep being her pen pal. I just don't have time to do all my schoolwork and write to two pen pals.

So long for now,
Reggie

Darn! Lisa thought, as she trudged from Booth to Fox Hall. Reggie really sounded serious about this new girl. Poor Kate! There must be something she could do to get them back together. After all, it wasn't butting in if she was doing something for their own good, was it? And they really made a perfect couple. They were both so intelligent.

Lisa let herself into Suite 3-D and dropped her books on the table by the door. Palmer was sprawled out on the pink loveseat, polishing her nails with Apricot Blush. Her makeup kit was open on the coffee table. Lisa peered into it thoughtfully.

"I hate it when I run out of liquid nail-dry," Palmer pouted, holding up the fingers of one hand and blowing gently across her nails. "The polish stays sticky forever."

"I think I have some in my room," Lisa offered.

"Really? Oh, Lisa, you're a lifesaver!" Palmer cried.

Lisa found the brush-on dryer in her top drawer and brought it back to Palmer. "Here, help yourself."

She watched while Palmer spread some of the clear liquid over her perfectly polished nails.

16

"I was just wondering," Lisa began hesitantly. "You're so good with makeup . . . do you think you could make someone who seemed, well, sort of plain look more glamorous?"

Palmer laughed and gave Lisa a superior look. "Of course I could. You ought to see what I did for Debby MacComber back home in Palm Beach. She was dying to make the cheerleaders last year, and . . ." Palmer fluttered her eyelashes. "Well, let's just say she's not what you'd call a natural beauty. When I was done with her, though, she looked like a movie star."

"Really?" Lisa grinned. "How did you do it?"

"It's just a small talent I have," Palmer said modestly.

"*What's* a talent?" Amy asked, walking into the sitting room with Shanon. They'd been listening to a new New Kids on the Block tape Amy had just gotten in the mail from a friend.

"How to use makeup," Lisa explained. "Listen, everyone, I have a fantastic idea. Let's do a major makeover on Kate."

"Oh," Amy groaned. "That's a bad pun. Get it? A major makeover on Kate *Majors*?

Shanon gave Lisa a searching look. "Then Reggie *did* dump her?"

Lisa nodded reluctantly. "He's writing to a girl named Cindy at Brier Hall."

"Oh, no!" the others wailed.

"She's not one of the Sisters, though. Anyway, I thought maybe if we helped Kate look a little better, Reggie might get interested in her again."

"I never thought the day would come when *you'd* want to help bring Kate and your brother together," Palmer said.

Lisa shrugged. "Better her than a Brier girl."

"True," Amy agreed.

"Let's go see if Kate's in her room now," Shanon suggested.

Palmer gave her nails one last critical glance and then carefully picked up her makeup case. "I'm ready. Let's go to work, Foxes!" But Lisa was already marching down the hall.

The other girls caught up with her outside Kate's door.

"Enter," Kate said flatly when Lisa knocked.

Kate didn't look as if she'd been crying this time, but she didn't look very happy either as the Foxes crowded into her single room.

"That's awfully nice of you," she said when she'd heard their plan, "but do you really think it will work? I mean, what if Reggie just doesn't like me anymore?"

"He does," Lisa assured her. "Come on. Let's start right now."

With an uneasy smile, Kate sat down in her desk chair and let Shanon drape a towel around her shoulders. Palmer spread an assortment of powder, blush, mascara, eyeliner, eye shadow, and half a dozen shades of lipstick out on the desktop.

While Kate fidgeted nervously in the chair, Palmer prepared to give her a totally new and devastatingly glamorous look. She worked slowly and carefully, and when she was finally finished the other girls stood back to admire her artistry.

"Well?" Kate asked, her voice cracking a little from nerves. "What do you think?"

18

"Mmm. I don't know . . ." Palmer tapped her chin with one long finger. "Something's missing."

"She's right," Lisa chimed in. "Your hair looks nice in that French braid. And the makeup is definitely flattering, but . . ."

In fact, Palmer's handiwork had done wonders. Kate's normally sallow skin was glowing pink, and Shanon had a feeling it wasn't just from the blusher. Her soft brown eyes sparkled brightly as Kate fluttered her newly mascaraed and surprisingly long lashes.

Lisa studied Kate approvingly. "I didn't realize you had such great eyelashes," she said.

"Take your glasses off," Palmer ordered suddenly.

"But I can't *see* without them," Kate complained.

"If she goes around bumping into walls and trees, Reggie won't be real impressed," Lisa pointed out.

"True," Palmer agreed, a slow smile forming on her own unlipsticked mouth. "But this is the nineties, girls. Modern science has provided alternatives for nearsightedness. They're called contact lenses!"

"Oh, no!" Kate breathed. "I don't think contacts are a very good idea. I've never tried them before. They seem awfully complicated—all those solutions and rules about how long you can leave them in and everything."

Lisa looked at her solemnly. "Well, it's up to you. If you don't really think Reggie is worth the trouble . . ."

Kate swallowed hard and looked up at Lisa earnestly. "Of course, I think he's worth it," she protested. "You *know* how much I like him!"

"Then it's settled," Palmer proclaimed with a graceful

19

flutter of her hands, as if she were Kate's fairy godmother, waving a magic wand. "All you have to do now is call and absolutely *beg* your parents to let you get contacts. If they send a letter giving you permission, you can get them fitted this weekend when we go to the mall."

Kate grinned. "Thanks, girls. I feel better already."

A few days later Shanon came bursting into Suite 3-D waving a square white envelope. "Look what I got," she squealed. "A letter from Mars!"

It had been well over a week since any of the girls had heard from their pen pals, and they all gathered around.

Shanon tore open the envelope, and her smile quickly faded.

"What's wrong?" Lisa asked. "What does Mars have to say?"

"Nothing," Shanon replied, studying a long sheet of legal paper. "It's just some sort of quiz Mars invented for his *know thyself* project."

"Wait a minute," said Amy, picking up the envelope. "There's something else in here."

Shanon eagerly snatched the envelope and unfolded a small piece of notepaper.

Dear Shanon,
　Hi! and how are you?
　Sorry I haven't written, but I've been too busy with this quiz. Could you take a look at it and let me know what you think? I'd be very interested to hear your opinion.

　　　　　　　　　　　　　　　　Your pal,
　　　　　　　　　　　　　　　　"Mars"

P.S. I hear Alma's having a Visitor's Day soon. Can't wait to see you!

"What kind of a quiz is he talking about?" Lisa asked. "It better not be anything to do with Latin!"

Shanon smiled, reading Mars's squiggly handwriting with some difficulty. "Don't worry. It's just supposed to help you type yourself as a preppy, a jock, or a dweeb. There's all kinds of questions about how you like to dress and the way you act around other people."

"That sounds silly," Palmer said.

"I think it sounds like fun," Amy disagreed, plopping down on the couch. "Go ahead, Shanon. Give us a sample question."

"Okay. Here's one: 'Say you get a roll at the dinner table. What do you do with it?' "

"Oh, this is really dumb," Palmer broke in. "You eat it, of course!"

"Wait a minute," Shanon laughed. "You didn't let me finish. You have to tell *how* you'd eat it. Would you break it in pieces and roll them into little bread balls, then pop them into your mouth? Would you cut it in half, butter each side, then stick them together again before eating the roll? Would you sop up gravy with it. Or would you throw it across the table?"

"And the answer to *that* is supposed to tell what type of person we are?" Palmer asked suspiciously.

"This is a riot!" Amy cried. "Okay, I'm game. I'd cut and butter it."

"Me, too," said Lisa.

21

Palmer let out an impatient sigh. "Well, given the choices—that's the only reasonable answer."

Shanon giggled. "I agree. Only, it might be sort of fun to make bread balls just once."

"So, what does the quiz have to say about all this?" Amy asked curiously.

Shanon skipped to the bottom of the page, where the scoring was explained. "According to this," she said, "you're a dweeb if you make bread balls. And if you cut and butter, you're a preppie."

"Then we're all preppies?" Amy said, tousling her spiky punk hairdo with a sly smile.

"I'll bet I know what the gravy soppers are," Palmer said, getting into the spirit of the game. "Jocks!"

"Right! But if you start a food fight, you don't fit into any of the categories," Lisa said, peering over Shanon's shoulder. "I guess Mars is still working on that one."

"I don't really think it's possible to type people just by their manners and their clothes," Shanon stated with a sigh. "But I'm not sure I should tell Mars that. It might hurt his feelings. It looks like he did a lot of work on this."

"Besides," Lisa said, "who can even remember how they eat rolls?"

"And only a real moron would throw food at the table," Palmer pronounced.

"That's not true," Lisa argued. "I once saw a full-fledged food fight when I was visiting Reggie at Ardsley. It was totally gross, but even the smartest boys were getting into it."

"Come on," Shanon urged. "Let's try more of the quiz."

22

All four Foxes took out paper and began marking down their answers to Mars's questions.

"I like this one," Lisa said. "How do you walk—toes pointed in? Toes pointed out? Or straight ahead?"

Amy looked thoughtfully at her feet. "I don't think I've ever watched my feet while I walk."

"How about this one?" Palmer asked. "If you are introduced to someone at a dance, do you say, 'Nice to meet you,' 'How do you do?' or do you just say 'Hi!'?"

" 'How do you do?' is definitely something *you'd* say, Palmer," Lisa commented.

"That sounds so stuffy," Amy complained, shaking her head. "A regular person would just say 'Hi!' "

Palmer shrugged. "I might say 'How do you do?' to adults, at one of my mother's parties. But not to other kids."

The girls compared notes when they'd finished taking the test. They all scored as preppies—even Amy.

"I wonder how our pen pals would answer the same questions," Lisa said.

"Let's take it again, pretending we're them," Amy suggested.

The others laughed, agreeing that would be fun. Lisa answered as if she were Rob, Shanon as if she were Mars, Amy for John, and Palmer for Sam.

When they were finished, they scored each other's quizzes and compared the results again.

Lisa giggled. "They're all preppies, too!"

"You can tell mostly by the way they dress," Shanon pointed out. "They all wear baggy pants, scuffed leather shoes, and loafers with no socks."

"I think there are different kinds of preppies," Palmer said seriously. "Rob is a preppie-jock because he likes sports. John is a preppie-dweeb, because he's sort of—"

"I've never seen Mars wearing loafers and no socks," Shanon broke in before Amy could object to Palmer's put-down of her pen pal. "Of course, I haven't seen him very many times at all, thanks to Alma's lack of interest in co-ed activities. But in Brighton at the public school where my sister Doreen went, the boys don't wear any shoelaces in their sneakers."

"Now *that*," said Palmer, "definitely falls into the roll-throwing category. It's just not civilized. In fact, it's totally barbaric! People who throw food and wear only part of their clothing are social animals!"

"That sounds as if they just enjoy socializing—you know, like 'party animals,' " said Amy.

"Whatever," Palmer said with a shrug. "I still think this whole thing is silly."

However, Shanon thought it was really pretty clever— like all of Mars's ideas. Before she went to bed that night she tore a piece of paper from her notebook and wrote:

Dear Mars,
We all liked your quiz. But we don't think the girls in 3-D can be typed. We're much too cool for that. However, we did come up with a new category—Social Animal! Maybe you could use it for your roll-throwers. What do you think?
You ought to submit your quiz to the Ardsley Lion. *I bet a lot of people would enjoy taking it.*

Indescribably yours,
Shanon

The following day the subject of Mars's quiz came up again at breakfast.

"I'd like to give that test to those obnoxious Sisters at Brier Hall," Lisa said through a mouthful of pancakes.

"Why bother?" Palmer grumbled. "They're all prepettes, just like they said in their ad—even though they have to *fake* it," she couldn't help adding. Then, with a frown, she daintily put down her fork and fixed her blue eyes unblinkingly on Amy.

"What's wrong?" Amy asked. "Why are you looking at me like that?"

"I've been thinking, and don't take this the wrong way, I'm just trying to be helpful," Palmer cautioned. "But maybe you should find a new hairstyle and stop dressing that way?"

"What way?" Amy said, looking hurt.

"Well . . ." Palmer searched for the appropriate words. "Like some sort of punk rocker. You know, John is as preppie as they come, Amy. If you're not careful, he may go looking for somebody who has more in common with him— like a certain prepette from Brier Hall." She raised a brow meaningfully.

"*Palm*-er!" Shanon cried indignantly. "I think Amy looks great this way."

Lisa put her arm around Amy's shoulder. "That's right. Amy shouldn't change for anyone. She's cool just the way she is."

"She's certainly cooler than any of those Sisters," Lisa seconded. "Amy has nothing to worry about from them. And neither do the rest of us."

But minutes later the Foxes got some news that made them all wonder. The four girls were just leaving the cafeteria when Brenda Smith, a fourth-former, came running up to them.

"Did you hear?" she asked breathlessly. "Brier Hall just announced that they're holding a four-week exchange program with the boys from Ardsley. At the end of the trial period, a committee's going to vote on whether Brier Hall will become *permanently* co-ed!" And without even waiting for their response, she hurried off to spread the word.

"Oh, no!" said Lisa as soon as Brenda was out of earshot. "This is serious."

"Brier Hall is the stuffiest school on the East Coast," Amy said in amazement. "Their headmistress is ten times stricter than Miss Pryn. I can't believe they're going to let *boys* in."

"It's just an experiment," Shanon reminded them. "Of course," she added with a gulp, "I guess every Ardie will want to get in on it."

"I'm glad Sam goes to Brighton," Palmer said. "He's so cute those Brier girls would be all over him. Not to mention his being such a fantastic drummer and—"

"Would you please stop thinking about yourself for once," Lisa snapped. "Don't you realize that the rest of us are in danger?"

Shanon's hazel eyes widened in alarm. "In danger? From what?"

"I think I know what Lisa means," Amy cut in. "If Ardsley is being asked to participate in this co-ed experiment, then maybe John—"

"*And* Rob, not to mention Mars," Lisa picked up, eyeing Shanon.

"I understand," Shanon said quietly. "If our pen pals get

into this program at Brier Hall, they may be too busy to write to us."

"Not only that," Lisa said, "but guess who they might run into?"

Palmer rolled her eyes. "The *fabulous* Sisters. Like I said, I'm glad Sam doesn't go to Ardsley."

"Oh, I don't think Mars and Rob and John would really want to go to Brier Hall," Shanon said, shaking her head. "Even though they kid around about Ardsley being like a military school, they really do like it."

"I wouldn't be so sure of that," said Lisa. "They might like the idea of being around girls for a change, too. Think how much they enjoy writing to us. Just imagine what *we'd* do if we had a chance to go to a boys' school for four weeks ourselves," she added.

"I'd definitely go," declared Palmer.

Amy looked at her. "Even if Sam wasn't there?"

Palmer shrugged. "Just because Sam is the number-one boy in my life at the moment, that doesn't mean I wouldn't enjoy meeting some other boys. Think how much more fun classes would be."

"Especially biology!" Amy giggled.

Shanon shook her head. "I sure hope our pen pals don't feel the same way about going to a girls' school," she said.

"There's only one way to find out," Amy declared. She gave Shanon and Lisa a look. "Let's write some letters."

CHAPTER 4

Dear Mars,

How are you? I am fine. Last week I had to read this short story I wrote for Mr. Griffith's English class out loud. The story was about a group of old musicians. I got the idea from my grandfather's mandolin group that meets on weekends. I was nervous reading the story, even though I was glad Mr. Griffith liked it.

Have you heard about the exchange program being offered at Brier Hall? It sounds interesting. I am wondering if you were interested in that, also. I told Lisa that you probably weren't, since you like Ardsley. Please write back.

Yours truly,
Shanon

Dear John,

Check it out. Brier Hall is having an exchange program. This is too weird, don't you agree? Imagine hanging around those Brier girls. Even I would not go to an exchange program over there. One thing I have learned since coming to Alma is that no matter how strict we are, Brier Hall is ten times stricter. Also, I heard through a friend of a friend that there is no music in the dorm after seven, even if you are in your own room and have the door shut. How is your music these days, by the way? I am still very much into New Kids on the Block. They are the best. Have you seen their latest video? I saw it on the dorm TV. I think I also heard that at Brier Hall there is no television allowed. Am I ever glad I go to Alma! I am sure you are glad you go to Ardsley.

Check you later,
Amy

Dear Rob,

I just happened to be thinking about you and thought I would write. What's happening over at Ardsley? Anything new? Did you hear that Alma's soccer team just beat Brier Hall's? I guess that they are not very good athletes over there. Brier Hall girls from what I know are definitely the dweeby type. I'm glad I decided to come to Alma, because it is very well-rounded and I like being around well-rounded people. Which, by the way, I think you are. Well-rounded, that is. Did you hear about the exchange program with Ardsley and Brier Hall by any chance? Even if you heard about it, I'm sure you wouldn't be interested. Right? I think about you a lot and have put your picture in a special place. Do you still have my picture?

Write soon,
Lisa

CHAPTER 5

Dear Lisa,

Where did you get the idea that all Brier girls are dweeby? Didn't you see that ad in the Ardsley *Lion with* those four girls who look like models? You must have missed it, because you couldn't say that all Brier girls were dweeby if you had seen that picture.

Congratulations on Alma winning the soccer match. I hear Brier is quite strong in tennis. Anyway, I'll soon be able to fill you in on what you don't know about Brier, because I am about to become a Brier girl myself. Ha, ha! I and the other Unknowns had definitely heard about the exchange program. There were not enough spaces for all the guys who practically camped outside the headmaster's office the morning the sign-up sheet for the program was put out. Anyway, John, Mars, and I didn't think we had a ghost of a chance, but we made it! Isn't that great?

We are looking forward to the change of scenery after

Ard-barf. The best part is that we won't even have to bike back and forth between the schools, because we got one of the dorm rooms at Brier. There were only a limited number of them. And The Unknown lucked out! The rooms at Brier are supposedly smaller than the ones we have at Ardsley. But it's okay with us. It's fun being in on an experiment. Whatever you have to say about Brier (I realize you have to not like the place since Brier and Alma are rivals), it is keeping up with the twentieth century, trying to go co-educational.

I have to sign off. I have a math assignment to finish, and then I have to pack my stuff for Brier.

Co-educationally yours,
Rob

"I don't believe it!" Lisa groaned, scrunching Rob's letter in her hands.

"It's bad enough that they're taking classes at Brier Hall—but living there?" Amy cried.

"A change of scenery," Lisa mumbled. "What's that supposed to mean?"

"Girls," Palmer interjected with a knowing nod. "That's all there is to see at Brier Hall. They're all over the place—especially in the dormitories."

"Maybe they're going to have special dorms for the boys," Shanon suggested hopefully, looking down at the unopened letter she'd just received from Mars.

"I wouldn't think so," Palmer said. "Remember what Rob said—'a limited number of rooms.' That doesn't sound like a whole separate building."

"She's right," Amy agreed miserably. "They probably have a couple of vacant rooms in each dorm."

"That's what co-ed is all about, girls," Palmer said philosophically.

Lisa's throat felt tight and scratchy. And just thinking about Rob living in the same building with the Sisters was making her stomach queasy. "I thought the boys and girls would just be going to classes together," she said, "not *living* together."

"Let's read the rest of our letters," Amy suggested. "Maybe they'll have more details."

Dear Amy,

I don't know where you got your information, but Brier Hall is not nearly as old-fashioned as you think. There are definitely TVs in every one of the dorms. And guess what? Mars, Rob, and I are going to be in the exchange program you mentioned. Good thing Brier didn't offer an exchange program with Alma, because if all the Alma girls feel the same way you do about Brier, nobody would sign up. Luckily, though, Brier has a super reputation at Ardsley. The academics are high there. And now Brier is becoming a pioneer in co-education. Well, not exactly a pioneer, since most of the other prep schools in the area are already co-ed. But they are definitely ahead of Alma in this area. And if the experiment works out okay, maybe even Alma will go co-ed and then you and I will be in class together. I will let you know about the music curfew at Brier. I probably won't mind if there is one, since I like it quiet when I am writing poetry. I usually only get into music in the morning. I agree

32

with you about New Kids on the Block—they're still the best group in this area or anywhere for that matter. I'll let you know how things are at Brier Hall. I have a feeling they will be delightful.

Your pen pal,
John

"*Delightful!*" Amy wailed. "I can't believe this! John was never interested in co-education before."

"What a bunch of baloney," Lisa said, shaking her long, dark hair. "By the time Alma goes co-ed, those Sisters will have stolen *our* pen pals!"

"Oh, come on," Shanon said. "Let's not get carried away. There's no reason to panic—yet," she added as she tore open her letter from Mars:

Dear Shanon,
Sorry I don't have much time to write. I'm busy finishing up my questionnaire. I also have two tests to study for tonight. Man, you should hear how excited everyone is over here at Ardsley. Guess you heard by now, The Unknown will be taking classes at Brier Hall for the next four weeks. I hear from John that it's a very good school. I just hope the food is better than here at Ardsley.

So long,
Mars

"Oh dear," Lisa murmured. "Mars's letter is no better than the others."

Shanon let out a long sigh. "How can he think about food at a time like this?"

"I just thought of something truly terrible," Amy said. "Mars's letter made me think of it. He signed off with *So long.*"

"So what?" Palmer exclaimed. "People say that all the time."

"You don't understand—it made me remember John's poem. Remember the acrostic?"

"F-A-R-E-W-E-L-L," Lisa spelled out the word.

"Farewell," Amy repeated mournfully. "Writing that poem *was* John's way of saying good-bye to me."

"I don't think John would drop you like that," Lisa said. "That would be cruel."

Palmer cleared her throat softly. "John *is* pretty deep," she said. "It might be his way of . . . well, breaking the news to Amy gently."

"Oh, I don't think so," Shanon said reassuringly. "Amy, I'm sure he would just say so."

"Boys aren't always logical," Palmer pronounced wisely. "Believe me, I've had much, much more experience than any of you."

"Well," Lisa said with conviction, "logical or not, it sounds to me like we're all about to get dumped. And I'm not about to take this lying down!"

"Speak for yourself," Palmer said breezily. "None of this has anything to do with Sam and me. I never thought I'd be glad he transferred from Ardsley to the Brighton public school, but I sure am now!"

"What are you going to do?" Shanon asked Lisa, ignoring Palmer's remark.

"I'm going to write straight back to Rob and ask him to try to convince the others not to go through with this stupid Brier Hall nonsense."

Amy gave Lisa a doubtful smile. "Do you really think that will work?"

Lisa smiled brightly back at Amy, and then at Shanon. "I'm sure it will," she said confidently. "You might as well read Sam's letter, Palmer. Maybe Mr. Rock Star can cheer us all up."

Dear Palmer,
I hope this letter reaches you in time—

"In time?" Amy interrupted. "This sounds serious!"
"Shush!" Lisa hissed, a finger across her lips. "Let her read!"

Palmer cleared her throat and continued.

I wanted to invite you to the Brighton basketball game this Saturday. We're playing Rockville, and it should be a great game. My father has volunteered to drive us. We could pick you up at six o'clock. Please send your answer right away to let me know if this is OK with you.

> *Yours truly,*
> *Sam*

"Ooooh, you're so lucky, Palmer," Lisa breathed.
"I know," Palmer said with a grin. "At least *one* pen pal knows how to be true."

Shanon and Amy looked at each other, then caught Lisa's eye, too. Sometimes Palmer's lack of sensitivity was just too much.

"I'd better go downstairs and get permission from Miss Grayson," Palmer said. Then she hurried out the door, her cheeks pink with excitement.

Minutes later, she was back with the good news: "Maggie said yes!" she cried, referring to Fox Hall's young resident faculty adviser by her first name, as the four Foxes often did—though never to her face. "I don't have to be back till ten!" Palmer added happily.

The afternoon of the Brighton game, Lisa, Amy, and Shanon went to the mall with Kate. Palmer refused to join them, even though they assured her they'd be back at Fox Hall long before Sam was due to pick her up.

Lisa marched right into Vincent Optical, with Amy and Shanon following close behind. But Kate hesitated at the door.

"I really don't know about this," she said nervously.

"You'll be fine," Lisa reassured her. "You have your parents' permission. Just think how nice it will be not to have to bother with glasses anymore."

"If I were you, I'd get tinted lenses," Amy said. "Purple. I've always wanted purple eyes."

Shanon looked at Amy in amazement. "Purple?"

"I just don't know," Kate repeated, even as the girls were shoving her through the door and up to the counter.

"May I help you?" a saleswoman with bright turquoise eyes asked.

Kate mumbled something about her glasses.

"She wants contacts," Lisa said, taking the note out of Kate's fingers and handing it to the woman.

"Well," she said, after reading the note, "looks as if all the necessary information is here. Let's get started fitting you, Kate. We have same-day service. So we should have you in your contacts within a couple of hours."

And by the time Shanon had visited the bookstore and Amy had checked out the record shop, Kate was wearing her new lenses.

"How do they feel?" Lisa asked as they stopped off at a snack bar for thick shakes before starting back to the school.

"Weird," Kate said uneasily. She reached up to rub her eyes.

"Don't do that!" Amy cried.

But it was too late. One of the lenses popped out.

"Don't anyone move," Kate cried. "I lost one of my contacts. Don't step on it! My father will kill me!"

"Here it is," Shanon said calmly. "Right under your seat." She gently picked up the clear little disk between two fingers and placed it in Kate's palm.

"I'd better wait to get back to Fox Hall to wash it off and put it back in," Kate decided.

The girls pedaled back to school in record time, and after leaving Kate at her door, they hurried straight to Suite 3-D to see how Palmer was doing.

Although Sam wasn't due to pick her up for another two hours, they found Palmer ready and waiting on the sitting-room loveseat. She was wearing a silky blue dress, just a shade darker than her eyes, low-heeled navy pumps, and a matching blue ribbon in her hair. Around her long, elegant neck was a single strand of pearls. "*Real* pearls," she said pointedly.

"You look beautiful," Shanon said, "but don't people usually wear jeans to a basketball game?"

Palmer gave her a haughty look. "Sam is *very* particular about clothes. I wouldn't dream of wearing anything as tacky as jeans to a social function at his school."

At exactly six o'clock Palmer said good night to her roommates and went downstairs alone to meet Sam. She timed it perfectly. His father's car was just pulling up in front of the dorm. Sam jumped out of the passenger side and ran up to the door where Palmer waited.

"Hi!" he said brightly, flashing her a wide smile. His reddish gold hair was neatly combed, and his gray eyes sparkled brightly. "Are you ready?"

"Yes." Palmer felt a pleasant flutter in the pit of her stomach. She had almost forgotten how handsome Sam was.

"You look really nice," Sam said, taking her hand to help her into the car.

"Thank you." Palmer knew she looked good, but it was still nice to hear Sam's compliment.

Then she glanced at Sam's outfit for the first time, and her heart almost stopped. He was wearing acid-washed jeans and a Brighton sweatshirt. On his feet were worn sneakers— without laces. And he wasn't wearing socks!

"You, um, you certainly are dressed . . . comfortably," she stammered, trying to be polite.

"Yeah, well . . ." He laughed. "These games are pretty casual."

"So I've heard," Palmer said grimly. Why hadn't she listened to Shanon and chosen something less conspicuous?

Oh, well, she supposed some other girls would be wearing dresses—or skirts, at least. Once they arrived at the game she'd feel better.

But as soon as Mr. O'Leary dropped them off in front of the gymnasium entrance of Sam's school, Palmer knew she'd made a major tactical error. The no-sock look was definitely in at Brighton. So were no shoelaces. *Everyone* was wearing jeans or chinos, even the girls. And *everyone* was staring at Palmer in her fancy party dress!

For a moment, Palmer felt like turning around and dashing out of the gym. But she forced herself to take a deep breath and calm down.

The important thing was that she was there on a date, a *real date*, with Sam. Palmer smiled and tossed her wavy blond hair. Nothing was going to spoil this date. Nothing!

They climbed into the bleachers and met a group of Sam's friends. He tried to introduce them, but Palmer couldn't hear a single name above the roar of the crowd. Already the cheerleaders were whipping up the fans, and the noise swelled each time the announcer introduced another team member over the P.A. system.

When the game started, Palmer leaned over to whisper in Sam's ear, "Thanks for inviting me."

"Huh?" He kept his eyes on the basketball court, following the Brighton player as he dribbled the ball.

"I said," she repeated more loudly, "thanks for asking me to come tonight!"

Sam shook his head and gave her a half grin. "No sense trying to talk here. Too noisy. And it'll only get worse before the game's over!" he said enthusiastically. "Isn't this great?"

"Terrific," Palmer muttered glumly. "Just the most romantic night of my life."

"*What?*" Sam shouted.

Palmer sighed. "Nothing."

Lisa looked up from the paperback book she was reading in bed and rubbed her eyes. It was almost ten o'clock and she was sleepy after the long bike ride to and from the mall, but she didn't want to turn in without hearing how Palmer's date had gone.

Just then the door from the hallway creaked open. Lisa sat up, suddenly wide awake. She grabbed her robe and tiptoed into the sitting room.

"Palmer! How was it?"

Startled, Palmer jumped and spun around. "Oh, it's you! You scared me half to death."

"Sorry." Lisa reached out and turned on a light. "Now"—she patted the cushion on the loveseat—"come tell me *everything*."

Palmer shrugged. "There isn't much to tell."

"Oh, come on," Lisa teased. "You went out on a real date with a gorgeous rock musician. Of course there's something to tell!"

"The score was eighty-six to seventy-two. Brighton won."

"Hey, that's great!" Lisa cried. "Sam must have been thrilled."

"I guess so," Palmer said flatly.

"Hey, what's wrong?" Lisa asked, suddenly concerned. Palmer shook her head dispiritedly. "It was so noisy during the game, Sam and I hardly got to say two words to each other all night long. And his father was waiting outside with the car the moment we left the gymnasium."

"Not very romantic," Lisa said.

"You've got that right. But the worst thing was my outfit—I was way overdressed. Everyone else was really casual. It was *so* humiliating! Sam will probably never ask me out again. His friends must have all thought I was really weird."

"Oh, I'm sure he'll ask you out again. Sam's not into clothes and all that stuff. I bet he didn't even notice how you were dressed."

"Do you really think so?" Palmer said, looking a little cheerier as she slipped out of the navy pumps and headed toward her room. "Where's Amy?" she asked.

"She and Shanon are down the hall trying to help Kate find her contact lenses. She keeps losing one or another of them."

"Good," Palmer said. "I think I'll write Sam a letter before I go to bed."

"That's an excellent idea," Lisa told her. "And I'll write one to Rob."

CHAPTER 6

Dear Sam,

Thank you for taking me to the game. I thought it was very interesting, and I liked being with you. I was surprised, though, that everyone was dressed so differently at Brighton. No socks in your sneakers. And no shoelaces. And everyone was so into the game and making a lot of noise and talking so much. Truly wild! I guess we're more formal at Alma. You Brightonites are just what some people would call social animals! Ha, ha. Anyway, thanks for the date.

Yours truly,
Palmer

Dear Palmer,

I was so steamed after I read your last letter, I couldn't wait to write back. I don't know where you get off calling my friends social animals. I like my friends just the way they are. Yes, we enjoy not dressing up. So what? Frankly, I was kind of surprised at what you wore to the basketball game.

My friends and I also like talking and laughing a lot. In other words, we like having fun and are not snobby. I don't know what your idea of having a good time is, but it's obviously very different from mine. Just because you're a preppy, that doesn't mean I have to be one, too. I'm me, and I'd appreciate it if you didn't try to make me something I'm not!

Sam

Dear Rob,

I thought you were my friend, but now you seem almost like a traitor, going to school at Brier Hall. You know that Brier Hall and Alma do not get along together. If I were you and Mars and John, I would not want to be like everybody else and go crazy about being in a co-ed program at Brier Hall.

Sincerely,
Lisa

P.S. I hear the food is terrible—mostly cauliflower and brussels sprouts.

Dear Lisa,

Excuse me for living! When I got your last letter, I read it over five times because I couldn't believe you would try to tell me what to do. Also, you're the one who goes to Alma, not me, so I don't see how you can call me a traitor. We are already at Brier Hall and the food is not all cauliflower or brussels sprouts.

Rob

Dear John,

I hope you have a good time at Brier. It sounds boring.

Yours truly,
Amy

Dear Amy,

I am at Brier and so far it is not boring. There is a lot to do getting acquainted with a new campus and different teachers. But the girls are really helpful. Everywhere you turn, there is another one trying to help us. Not only that, we each have an individual girl sponsor. You should get to know some Brier girls. They are nice people. I don't think it's too cool of you to call the place boring when you haven't even been here. I have to go now. My sponsor is waiting to take me to art class.

Sincerely,
John

Dear Mars,

I hope you have fun at Brier Hall. Where should I send your letters? I hope you get this one.

Fondly,
Shanon

Dear Shanon,

Surprise! I am already at Brier Hall. All the guys are staying on one floor of this incredibly old-fashioned dormitory. John, Rob, and I are sharing this one room that looks as if it was made for midgets. Other than that, things are incredibly interesting so far. Have you seen this article

44

*that was in the Brighton News? Brier is getting a lot of
publicity, thanks to these four girls who call themselves the
Sisters. By the way, I have seen them. In fact, Paige McGraw
is in one of my classes here at Brier. They look even more
like models in person than they do in their newspaper
pictures. Anyway, Rob, John, and I have read this article
about them that was in the newspaper and we get to see them
every day in person, so I thought I'd send the clipping to you.
Did you and the Foxes get your original idea for advertising
for pen pals from the Sisters?*

*Your wild and crazy pen pal,
Mars*

"Can you *believe* this?" Lisa cried.

"It's unbelievable!" said Amy, pacing the carpet. "Those
. . . rats!"

"Mars isn't a rat," Shanon protested.

"Neither is Sam," said Palmer. "He just doesn't understand me!"

"I'm not talking about Mars or Sam," moaned Lisa. "I'm
talking about this newspaper article! The nerve of those
Brier Hall girls, stealing our idea about pen pals and then
taking all the credit for it. That's out-and-out lying!"

"I agree!" said Amy. She stared at the newspaper clipping
that Mars had sent Shanon. "Imagine that Paige person
saying the idea of advertising for boy pen pals at Ardsley was
originally theirs!"

"When everybody in the world knows it was ours!"
spluttered Lisa. "We put our ad for pen pals in the Ardsley
Lion months ago! They just put theirs in this spring."

Shanon took the article from Amy and read it again. The Brighton newspaper certainly had treated the four Brier girls like celebrities. Beneath the flattering picture of Paige McGraw and her three friends—Patricia Sloane, Angelique Medina, and Brooke Baines—was a short article about the girls, tying them in with the recent co-ed experiment at their school. Shanon's eye zoned in on the quote from Paige McGraw, who was clearly the Sisters' leader:

"We wanted to meet boys and since we're an all-girls' school, we thought up a very original idea of advertising for boy pen pals. Now, of course, everybody is doing it. I hear a group of Alma Stephens girls are advertising for boy pen pals. We're glad they liked our idea. . . ."

"What a fairy tale!" Lisa exploded. "What a made-up story! Those girls *stole* our idea!"

"Maybe they didn't see our ad last fall," Shanon suggested.

"I bet they did," Amy argued. "You can tell that Paige girl knows about us. That group of Alma girls she mentioned has got to be us! Remember how famous we got when we ran that ad at Ardsley?"

"Not as famous as the Sisters," Palmer said with a sigh. "Nobody from the Brighton *News* came to interview *us* or take *our* picture."

"Probably the only reason the paper interviewed them is this new co-ed program at Brier Hall," reasoned Shanon. "There's nothing we can do about it, anyway."

"I know," Lisa muttered. "But it still isn't fair. Did you

read that part about how they don't accept just *anybody* for their pen pals?" she added sarcastically.

Shanon giggled. "It *was* pretty snooty." She stuck her nose in the air and read aloud from the article. " 'We don't take just *any*body for a pen pal,' Paige McGraw said. 'First of all, the boys must be good in academics. We also must see their pictures before we will write to them.' "

Lisa laughed. "Academics! What a laugh! Well, that lets Rob out. He's certainly not an A student."

"True," said Amy, "but his picture would more than make up for his grades, I bet."

"Don't *say* that!" Lisa pleaded. "I really like Rob. And I like being his pen pal. I don't want him writing to those Sisters."

"He won't have to write to them," Palmer said grimly. "Now that he's going to school with them, he can talk to them in person. He won't even have to pick up a telephone."

A moment of worried silence filled Suite 3-D.

"Let's not think about it," Amy said, getting up suddenly. She grabbed her guitar. "If The Unknown get to be friends with the Sisters, so what? Anyway, there's nothing we can do about it."

"I guess not," sighed Lisa. "I just wish Rob wasn't at Brier Hall."

"Well, if you think your situation is rough," said Palmer, "don't forget the letter Sam wrote to me."

"He really did sound upset," Shanon agreed.

"He totally misunderstood me," Palmer said. "I didn't mean to call anybody a *real* animal when I said he and his friends were *social* animals."

47

"Maybe you should write him and explain," Shanon suggested.

"Maybe we should *all* write to our pen pals," said Lisa. "That way, even though they're at Brier Hall, they'll think of us."

Suddenly there was a frantic knocking at the door; and before anyone could say, "Come in," Kate Majors burst into the suite. "You've got to help me!" she cried.

The other girls gathered around her. "What's the matter?" Shanon asked sympathetically. "You look like you just lost your best friend."

"Just like the rest of us," quipped Lisa.

"It's not my best friend," Kate sniffed, "it's my contact lens. It popped out and I can't find it anywhere! I must have been crazy to get those awful things. They're nothing but trouble."

"Calm down," Shanon said. "We'll help you find it."

"Sure we will," said Amy.

"And after that," said Lisa, "we'll figure out what to do about *our* problem."

Dear Rob,
Sorry you think I was trying to tell you what to do.
                                                   Yours truly,
                                                   Lisa

Dear John,
Hope you enjoy the academics at Brier Hall.
                                                   Sincerely,
                                                   Amy

48

Dear Mars,

I got your letter, and I am glad you are having fun at Brier Hall. We did not get our idea to advertise for boy pen pals from the Sisters. Write soon.

Yours,
Shanon

Dear Sam,

I do not want to make you into something you aren't. And I couldn't care less whether or not you wear shoelaces.

Love,
Palmer

CHAPTER 7

———◆———

Lisa, Amy, Shanon, and Palmer sat in the library reading room. Lisa gazed disinterestedly at the floor-to-ceiling bookshelves that lined the dark green walls. Normally this was one of her favorite places on campus, but tonight she just didn't have the heart for book browsing.

In fact, though they all had textbooks opened up in front of them, none of the Foxes was actually reading.

Finally, Palmer glanced up from her history text and slapped it closed. "I give up! I simply can't concentrate. It's been over a week since I wrote to Sam, and he hasn't answered."

"Do you think he's still mad at you for calling him a social animal?" Shanon asked in a whisper.

"I don't know," Palmer said with a sigh. "I thought I apologized."

"Maybe he didn't read your letter," Lisa pointed out. "Maybe he was too mad to."

Amy nodded. "That's one possibility. Maybe he tore Palmer's letter up without even reading it."

"Boys!" Palmer groaned, a little louder than she planned.

The school librarian looked up from her desk at the far end of the room with a displeased frown.

"Boys can be so stubborn sometimes," Palmer added in a lower voice.

"What about the rest of our pen pals?" Shanon asked. "Do you think they're *all* mad at us? By now they've had plenty of time to answer our letters."

"Mars has nothing to be upset about, and neither does John," Amy stated.

"Rob *was* pretty upset when I told him I didn't think he should enroll in the exchange program," Lisa admitted sadly. "But I didn't think he was angry enough to stop writing."

"Maybe," Amy said slowly, "they aren't getting our letters."

"Why wouldn't they get them?" Lisa asked. "We're sending them directly to Brier Hall."

"You never know," Amy said with a shrug. "There could be a mix-up in their mail room. Maybe the people who sort the mail don't know which rooms the boys are in. That would at least explain why we haven't heard from them."

"True . . ." Palmer agreed slowly. "But there could be another explanation."

"What?" the other three echoed, trying to keep their voices down.

"Rob, John, and Mars might be too busy making friends with the Brier Hall girls—maybe even those sneaky Sisters!"

51

"Oh, no!" Shanon gasped.

Lisa bit her lip. "I hate to even say it, but Palmer might be right. I hear the Sisters are the big news at Ardsley these days. All the boys are dying to meet them."

"How'd you hear that?" Amy demanded.

"Reggie," said Lisa, pulling out a folded piece of lined notebook paper.

Dear Lisa,

I thought I'd be a good brother and write to you again, since you like getting my letters so much. Anyway, I've just moved in at Brier Hall, and I think this place is going to be super!

The school has gone out of its way to make us feel right at home. Each of the boys has a sponsor who takes him around to classes to make sure he doesn't get lost the first few days. And they're having a special reception for the Ardsley students tomorrow night with refreshments and a film afterward.

Everyone back at Ardsley who didn't get accepted into the Brier program is really jealous. Guys were literally drooling over that photograph of the Sisters. And here they're just about the most popular girls on campus.

Anyway, since you're so interested in Brier, I'll try to write more often and keep you posted on all the neat things happening here.

> *Your brother,*
> *Reggie*

"Maybe he's just teasing you," Shanon said hopefully.

"Probably some of his enthusiasm is a put-on," Lisa admitted. "But it's hard to say how much."

For a long while, no one said a thing.

"Well, what do we do now?" Shanon asked at last.

"I say we write them one more time, in a group letter," Amy suggested.

"I guess I'll write to Sam again, too," Palmer said.

That night, Lisa, Amy, and Shanon huddled over the sitting-room desk. The letter-writing process took a very long time. But on the fifth try the three girls were finally satisfied. The letter was short but direct and to the point.

Dear Unknowns,
 Why haven't you answered our letters? Are we still pen pals?

> *Yours truly,*
> *Foxes of the Third Dimension*

After Lisa, Amy, and Shanon had composed their short message to Rob, John, and Mars, they helped Palmer write to Sam.

Dear Sam,
 I think it is good to have fun also. I am sorry if you think I was being snooty.

> *Yours truly,*
> *Palmer Durand*

CHAPTER 8

———◆———

Exactly one week later, the occupants of Suite 3-D called an emergency meeting to discuss their pen pal situation.

Shanon sat quietly on the pink loveseat, chewing on a fingernail.

Palmer stood in front of the mirror, admiring the new sequined sweater her mother had just sent her from Palm Beach.

Amy and Lisa sat side by side on the floor.

"I think," Lisa began, "the time has come for action with a capital A!"

Palmer spun around and looked down her nose at Lisa. "What do you suggest? We've already written them. We can't call them on the phone. You don't have the number for the Unknowns' Brier Hall dorm—and after the way Sam's ignored my letters, I wouldn't dream of calling *him*!"

"What else can we do?" Shanon said miserably.

"The only way to find out what's going on with the boys is to check things out *in person*," Lisa said firmly.

"Oh, sure, and how are you going to do that?" Palmer demanded. "Just tell Miss Pryn we've decided to switch schools for a week?"

"No," Lisa said with a mischievous smile. "I have a much better idea. I just saw an interesting notice on the bulletin board. The Brier Hall orchestra is giving a concert this weekend. Students from all the nearby schools are invited. All we have to do to get tickets is sign up at the administration office."

Amy let out a little yip of excitement. "That's a *great* plan! We'll go to the concert, and while we're on the Brier Hall campus, we can scout out the situation."

"Let's invite Kate, too," Shanon suggested. "I'm sure she'd love the chance to see Reggie!"

"Okay!" Lisa said, grinning at her friends' enthusiasm. "Let's go ask her now."

All four girls streaked down the third-floor hallway. Amy was the first to Kate's door, which she pounded on with great energy. When the fifth-former opened it, they piled into her room uninvited.

"Guess what?" Amy gasped breathlessly. "We've thought of a way for you to see Reggie!"

Kate's pale cheeks turned bright pink. "You have?"

"Well," Lisa corrected, "it doesn't exactly *guarantee* you'll get to see him. But you'll at least be able to go to Brier Hall with us . . . and there's always a chance."

"Oh, you mean the concert," Kate said glumly, collapsing onto her bed. "I heard about it."

"You do want to go, don't you?" Palmer asked. "It's the perfect opportunity for Reggie to see the new you."

Kate chewed her lip, thinking. "No. I just can't do it."

"Why not?" Amy demanded.

Kate shrugged. "I wouldn't feel right, chasing after Reggie like that."

"What do you mean?" Lisa said. "We're just going to hear a concert. It's all perfectly innocent."

Kate grimaced. "I'd just be too embarrassed if he showed up and thought I was there just to see him. And he might, you know. It would be sort of obvious."

"Maybe Kate's right," Shanon murmured worriedly. "After all, we've never gone to a Brier Hall concert before. Won't it seem kind of strange if we do bump into the Unknowns?"

"Don't be silly," Lisa said calmly. "Bumping into them is the whole point. Besides, chances are they won't even be at the concert."

"Right," Amy agreed. "We're just going to hear some good music, pick up some information, maybe talk to a few Brier Hall students, ask them about the new program and if they know our pen pals."

"And if the boys do happen to be there, we'll just pretend we don't see them. In fact"—Lisa's brown eyes twinkled—"if we work this right, *they'll* spot *us* and come over to talk."

"Perfect!" Amy cried.

Shanon hesitated a moment, then nodded slowly. "I suppose that would be nice. Then I'd be able to ask Mars in person why he hasn't written. I think I'd rather hear the truth, even if it is bad news."

"Well, good luck to you," Kate said doubtfully, "but I think I'll pass on this."

The night of the concert, Miss Grayson had announced that she and Mr. Griffith would be waiting outside Fox Hall at 6:15 p.m. in the Alma van. The two teachers would drive the girls to Brier Hall.

The Foxes dressed especially carefully that night—just in case they did run into their pen pals. Lisa chose a purple and lime green jumpsuit with a matching green butterfly clip for her hair. Amy wore a short black tube dress with a silver belt and dangling rhinestone earrings. Shanon changed four times before she was finally satisfied with the soft heather sweater and pants she put on at last. And Palmer, who was going along for moral support even though Sam wouldn't be there, wore her best navy blue blazer and a coordinated skirt and blouse.

The Foxes settled down on the long back seat of the Alma van and immediately began whispering among themselves. There were five other girls in the van, but true to her word, Kate Majors was not one of them.

"I heard Miss Grayson say something about a reception," Lisa whispered.

"Really?" Amy grinned. "I bet she meant a *wedding* reception."

"It could mean anything," Palmer put in knowingly. "There are all kinds of receptions. I've been to absolutely hundreds of them."

Shanon giggled. "I've only been to one kind—the wedding kind. I bet that's what they're talking about. I wonder if we'll be invited."

Ever since Maggie Grayson, the pretty young French

teacher, and Dan Griffith, the handsome young English teacher, had announced their engagement, the girls had speculated excitedly about wedding plans.

"Of course we'll be invited," Lisa said, sure of herself on this count. "We have Mr. Griffith for English. And Miss Grayson is our dorm faculty adviser."

"Don't get your heart set on it," Palmer advised. "They might have a small, intimate wedding and invite only a few close friends."

"Oh," Shanon groaned, clearly disappointed. "I hope not. I'd give anything to see Miss Grayson in a wedding gown, all lace and pearls. I bet she'll look beautiful."

All the way to Brier Hall the girls were busy gossiping about possible wedding plans, but when the van swung between the huge stone pillars marking the drive onto the campus they turned silent.

Lisa felt as if her heart was only hitting every other beat, and her stomach twisted up in a knot. What if the boys weren't there? she thought nervously. And then, even more nervous-making, what if they *were* there?

Slowly the Foxes climbed down from the van, the last ones out. Miss Grayson was already waiting at the back door.

"Dan," she called to Mr. Griffith, "I'll stay here with the girls if you'll park the van."

"Right, Maggie," he said with a wink, which made all the Alma girls giggle. "I'll find you inside."

"Does everyone have a ticket?" Miss Grayson asked, doing her best to ignore the girls' titters.

"Yes," they all answered at once.

"Good. There are no reserved seats, so you may sit any-where you like," the teacher said. "Have fun," she added as everyone hurried off to the auditorium.

Inside, the houselights were still on. The four Foxes stood behind the back row, scanning the audience, most of which was already seated.

"See anyone you know?" Palmer asked archly.

"Not yet," Amy said, her dark eyes darting around the room.

"Oh, wait." Shanon reached out to squeeze Lisa's arm. "Isn't that Reggie? Over on the left side, about four rows from the back?"

Lisa squinted, searching the section where Shanon was pointing.

"That's him," she announced, surprised to see he was sitting alone. "I wonder where his new pen pal, Cindy, is."

"Maybe she isn't musical," Shanon said.

"Or maybe she's just late," Palmer suggested. "Come on, now is our chance. Before she shows up, let's ask Reggie to point out the competition."

"You mean the Sisters?" Lisa asked.

"Exactly," Palmer said. "We might as well see what they look like in person. Maybe that photo we saw was totally flattering. Maybe they really look just like regular girls!"

Walking in pairs with Lisa and Palmer up front, the Foxes made their way down the aisle toward Reggie. All four slid into the row beside him.

He turned with a startled look on his face when Lisa pinched his arm. "What are you doing here?" he asked.

"We came for the concert," she said lightly.

He gave her a critical frown. "Is that so?"

"Well," she admitted, unable to actually lie to her brother, "there might be some additional reasons."

"Four of them," Amy giggled meaningfully.

Reggie laughed. "You mean the famous Sisters?"

"Something like that," Lisa said. "We're just curious to see what they look like in person."

Reggie shook his head. "Leave it to my sweet sister to cook up something like this." He scanned the rows of heads to his right, then down toward the front of the auditorium. "Well, you don't have to look far," he said, indicating a group of girls with a tilt of his head. "There they are, sitting together."

Lisa followed his gesture.

Indeed, there were four girls, dressed almost exactly alike in pretty pastel cardigans and pearl necklaces, their long hair combed smooth and straight down their backs. But it wasn't the girls who really caught her eye, it was the three boys spaced between them.

Lisa felt the blood rush to her face as she recognized John, Mars, and Rob. The three boys were laughing and whispering with the girls as if they were having the time of their lives—which Lisa most definitely *was not*!

CHAPTER 9

———◆———

Lisa couldn't believe her eyes. "Look!" she hissed, nudging Amy with an elbow.

In the next instant, first Amy and then the other girls spotted their pen pals. Their faces froze in shock, and no one said a word.

Finally, Shanon broke the silence. "Oh my gosh," she gasped. "It's The Unknown! What do we do now?!"

"There are two possibilities as I see it, Foxes," Palmer said coolly. "Either we turn around and walk out of here without the boys ever realizing we were here, or we try to move closer so we can catch some of their conversation. Maybe things aren't as bad as they look."

"But what if they *see* us?" Shanon asked, amazed at Palmer's boldness.

"Palmer's right," Lisa agreed after some thought. "We don't really know what's going on."

"It seems pretty clear to me," Lisa muttered. "Look at the way they're all laughing and fooling around."

"Oh, I don't know," Palmer said. "Maybe those sneaky

Sisters followed the boys to their seats and arranged to sit with them. Maybe it has nothing to do with what Rob, John, and Mars wanted."

"I wouldn't put it past them," Amy declared.

"But what if we find out the boys really like *them* better than they like *us*?" Shanon asked, looking forlorn.

Lisa looked at Amy, then Palmer, and back to Shanon. "I guess then we'll know we've lost our pen pals," she said sadly.

"I think I'd rather not know," Shanon said. "I think we should get out of here before it's too late."

"Don't be such a scaredy cat," Lisa said. She hesitated a minute, glancing at Reggie, who she was sure wouldn't approve of their plan. "Come on," she whispered, pulling Shanon to her feet. "We've come this far—we might as well see what's up."

Reggie shook a warning finger at his sister. "You're asking for trouble, Lisa."

She drew a deep breath and, ignoring him, began to inch her way past the other girls and out of the row of auditorium seats. Shanon, Palmer, and Amy followed.

Lisa's heart thumped as they hurried down the auditorium aisle. By now, the students and parents all appeared to have settled into their seats, waiting for the concert to begin. Still, there was plenty of room in a number of spots. Just two rows behind the boys from Ardsley were four vacant seats.

Lisa headed straight for them.

An elderly couple, probably someone's grandparents, were sitting between the Foxes and the Unknowns. They were talking quietly, but Lisa was pretty sure she'd be able to hear over them, and she was right.

One of the Sisters was telling the boys about her shopping trip to the mall. "You wouldn't believe what junk they have in those stores," she exclaimed loudly.

"I know," said one of the other girls. "I couldn't find *anything* good enough for the dance coming up here next month. I don't know how the townies can stand it."

Amy was sure they were hinting that they wanted dates.

"What a snob!" Palmer hissed, and Amy gave her a wry look. Snobbism was something Palmer had been accused of more than once herself!

Lisa ignored them both. All her attention was fixed on the back of Rob's head.

Just then, the worst thing that could have possibly happened did happen. Shanon got the hiccups.

Lisa, Palmer, and Amy stared at their suitemate in horror as Shanon's nervous hiccups got too loud and unpredictable to stifle.

Amy jumped to her feet, pulling Shanon up with her, and began pushing her way out of the row.

Lisa and Palmer hastily rose, too. But before any of the Fox Hall girls could move more than a few feet, Mars turned around to see what the commotion was about. And then the other boys and the Brier girls were staring, too.

I am going to *die*! Lisa thought miserably as Rob's eyes locked with hers. Lisa knew she had to say something, but before she could figure out what, the houselights dimmed and the curtain rose on the Brier Hall orchestra.

"Sit down," someone in a row behind the girls commanded harshly. "Sit down, please!"

Shanon's hiccups stopped almost immediately, undoubtedly scared out of her by the shocked look on Mars's face.

Unsure of what to do, Palmer sat down abruptly. Lisa and Amy exchanged horrified looks and sat also.

The conductor gave the downbeat, and the slow sweet strains of Debussy's *Clair de Lune* filled the room. But the beautiful music was wasted on the four Foxes.

Even Amy, the music lover, didn't hear a single note. All she could think of was John. What could he possibly be thinking now?

Beside Amy, Shanon sank down in her seat, wishing she'd never agreed to come to the concert. And Lisa felt like a total fool. Even Palmer was beginning to wish she'd stayed at the dorm. After all, *her* pen pal didn't even know the Brier Hall girls.

The minute the houselights came up again, Lisa jumped from her seat and made a mad dash for the nearest exit. The other girls tore after her.

Back at Fox Hall, the four girls huddled around the coffee table. "Tonight was the absolute worst night of my life!" Lisa wailed.

"It *was* pretty awful," Amy agreed. "And we still don't know for sure what's going on. We've *got* to find out whose idea it was to sit with those Brier Hall snobs. The only solution is to write a letter to the boys, tonight!"

"Oh, no!" Shanon groaned. "I don't think we ought to. I mean, what would we say? We can't come right out and *ask* them if they were on a date!"

"It sure looked that way," Palmer said, a little too calmly for Amy's taste. Palmer wouldn't be so cool if Sam had been sitting with those Sisters!

"I have an idea," Lisa said thoughtfully. She pulled a piece of paper toward her, and tugged off the top of her pen with her teeth.

Hi guys,

Sorry we didn't get a chance to say hello tonight. The Alma van was leaving right after the concert. We were surprised to see you there. In fact, we didn't even notice you until the lights were almost ready to go off.

We were just wondering who those preppie girls sitting near you were? Are they friends of yours from Brier Hall? We'd certainly like to meet them if they are. Maybe you could find pen pals for them at Ardsley.

Your best *friends,*
The Foxes of the Third Dimension

"What do you think?" Lisa asked, leaning back to take a critical look at her work.

"It's important that it doesn't sound nasty . . . like you're jealous or anything," Palmer pointed out. "That's good."

"Do you think the boys will believe that bit about not noticing them?" Amy asked, frowning.

"Why not?" Lisa said. "At least this way, it might seem like chance that we chose seats two rows behind them."

"I like the part about reminding them we're their pen pals and suggesting they get those other girls pen pals of their own," Shanon said firmly. "It's *very* clever!"

Three days later, Amy returned from her classes with the mail. The other girls were already in the suite.

65

"There's a letter from Brier Hall!" she shouted, crashing through the door to the sitting room.

Lisa good-naturedly snapped it out of her hand. "I get to read it out loud since I wrote the letter to them."

Dear Foxes,

Hope you enjoyed the concert as much as we did. It sure was nice—and what a surprise to see you there!

We're a little confused, though. You said in your letter that you didn't know we were there. But after you left, we bumped into Reggie and he made some joke about you girls "checking up" on us.

There must be some explanation. And we can only think of one—that you were spying on us. That would be pretty sly—but sort of beneath Foxes, don't you think?

Please respond.

> *Needing to know,*
> *The Unknown (Rob, John, and Mars)*

"Oh, dear!" Shanon wailed. "I *knew* we shouldn't have gone to Brier. Now they think we were *spying* on them!"

"How could they say such a thing?" Lisa moaned. "All we wanted to do was *talk* to them."

"Palmer, you always know what to do," Amy said hopefully. "Tell us how we can get back our pen pals."

"Sorry, I have problems of my own," Palmer replied absently.

"Not as bad as ours," Amy insisted.

Palmer laughed. "Wrong again. I have to somehow convince Sam that I'm not the kind of snobby girl who judges guys on whether or not they tie their sneakers."

"That's *easy*," Amy said briskly. "All you have to do is send him a copy of Mars's questionnaire."

Palmer beamed at her roommate. "Hey, thanks, Amy. That's a great idea, and it's just what I'll do."

CHAPTER 10

───◆───

Dear Sam,

I think what we have here is just a silly misunderstanding. Enclosed please find a copy of a questionnaire Mars sent to my suitemate Shanon. We were playing around with it, trying to figure out what category each of us—and each of our pen pals—fits into.

Well, I always assumed you were a preppie. I was just surprised when we went to the game that you were behaving so un-preppie-ish. So, you see, there's nothing to be upset about.

Your pen pal,
Palmer

Dear Palmer,

Let's get one thing straight: I'm not a preppie, and I never have been. I've always hated that style, which is one reason why I left Ardsley. As far as I'm concerned, people who try to copy the preppie style are stuck-up snobs.

68

I'm not saying that everyone *who's like that is a fake. But most of them are, and I don't want any part of it. I guess you're comfortable with the way you dress, and I suppose that it's sort of the preppie look—but it suits you. It's not me, though. So please quit trying to make me over.*

Seriously,
Sam

Dear Sam,

Since you're so against preppies and prepettes, maybe it's a mistake for us to continue as pen pals. We're just so different, and I don't want to change just to please someone who can't recognize style when he sees it!

And by the way, Sam, I'm not the snob. You are!

I was only teasing when I wrote to you after the basketball game. "Social animals" was just a name for people who like to socialize, to have a good time. Your friends seemed to be like that. I don't care what they wear, or what you wear, not really. But you decide you don't like someone just because they wear preppie stuff. That sounds like a super snob to me!

Don't bother writing to me anymore.

Good-bye,
Palmer

CHAPTER 11

Kate Majors knocked on the door of Suite 3-D.

"Come in," a dreary voice invited.

Slowly, Kate opened the door and peered inside.

Lisa was lying on the pink loveseat, one arm thrown up over her eyes. Amy and Shanon were sprawled on the floor, chins wedged on folded arms. Palmer stood behind them, staring morosely out the window.

"What's wrong?" Kate asked. "Did someone die or something?"

"We're not in mourning," Palmer said irritably. "We're just *mad!*"

"Actually," Lisa added, not bothering to peek out from beneath her arm, "we're past being mad—we're plotting revenge."

"Revenge against whom?" Kate asked, sitting down on the floor beside Shanon.

"The Sisters at Brier Hall," Shanon said with unusual fervor. "Our pen pals have stopped writing altogether.

70

Those Sisters not only stole our *idea* for advertising for pen pals, they stole our pen pals!"

"We have to take emergency action," Amy chimed in.

"I don't see that there's anything you can do," Kate commented after a moment's thought.

"Well, I do," said Lisa, producing a carefully folded sheet of blue paper.

Kate glanced at the brief note on Lisa's stationery:

Dear Sisters,

We are a group of girls at Alma Stephens who call our-selves Foxes of the Third Dimension. We put an ad in the Ardsley Lion *last fall advertising for boy pen pals. We are wondering if you saw our ad. If you got your idea for advertising for pen pals from us, it is okay. Only we think it is only fair that the next time you are interviewed by a newspaper you give us credit for the idea of boy pen pals from Ardsley also. This is only fair.*

Yours truly,

Foxes of the Third Dimension

P.S. Please write to us in care of the Alma Stephens Ledger.

"Wow," said Kate. "That's pretty heavy. Are you really going to send it?"

"Of course," said Lisa. "We just want to get things straight."

"It's the principle of the thing," Amy added. "People shouldn't steal other people's ideas and then get away with it."

"It's awfully brave of you," Kate said admiringly.

"You notice that we didn't sign our real names," Shanon added hastily. "We wouldn't want those girls picking a fight with us or anything. Still, if they *do* get interviewed again—"

"They should say that they got their idea from the Foxes of the Third Dimension," Lisa added proudly.

Kate turned to leave. "Great. Well, I'm glad you've found a way to solve your problem."

"That's not all we're going to do," Amy added, blocking Kate at the doorway. "We're going to solve *your* problem, too."

"My problem?" Kate asked.

"Sure," said Lisa eagerly. "Reggie! We've got a great idea that will help get all our pen pals—*and* yours—back. All you have to do is—"

"Wait a minute," Kate interrupted. "If Reggie doesn't like me anymore, I'm not going to make a fool of myself running after him."

"I didn't say anything about running after him," Lisa objected, suddenly sitting up straight. "Besides, he still hasn't seen the new you. I bet he'll have second thoughts once he gets a look at your new hairdo and makeup. All you have to do is go to Brier Hall . . . on newspaper business."

Kate narrowed her eyes. "*What* newspaper business?"

Lisa smiled mysteriously. "You're going to interview Rob Williams and his roommates about their experiences in the exchange program. We'll supply the questions. That way we'll find out for sure what's going on there."

"What makes you think they'll agree to an interview with one of your friends?" Kate asked.

"They're not going to know that you have anything to do

72

with us," Lisa said quickly. "You can write to Rob asking for the interview. Just say you're in town for a short time . . . that you're from some foreign country."

Lisa stared off into space, trying to think of a likely birthplace for Kate.

"I know!" Amy exclaimed. "She can be from Australia. It's an English-speaking country. Since I used to live there, I can help her fake the accent!"

"Super!" Lisa squealed, dashing over to the desk the four girls shared and pulling out some plain white stationery.

"Here, Kate. I'll dictate and you write down everything I say. Rob might recognize my handwriting. We'll just make the letter short and official-sounding."

"This will never work," Kate moaned.

"Of course it will!" Lisa assured her with a bright smile. "What can possibly go wrong?"

Dear Master Robert Williams,

Let me introduce myself. I am a reporter for my school newspaper in Sydney, Australia. I am spending this semester in America, at the Alma Stephens School for girls, through a foreign exchange program sponsored by the International Journalism Club. I heard about your participation in the Brier Hall co-education experiment and would like to interview you and some of your friends concerning your feelings on the subject.

We are particularly interested to see how this works in a small private school. Your personal experiences might also be of interest to my readers, since they are the same age as you but live on the other side of the world.

If you are interested, please write to me in care of—

"What should we put for an address?" Lisa asked. "We can't have him send his answer to *us*."

"That's right," Shanon said uneasily. "There's no way we can get his answer without giving ourselves away."

"Wait a minute," said Kate, letting herself get swept up in the scheme. "I have an idea. We can have them send it *in care of the Journalism Club, Alma Stephens School*. I'll watch the club's mail and bring their answer to you when it comes," she offered with a grin. "And I'd better use a fake name, to make sure they don't recognize mine."

"Perfect!" Lisa exclaimed. "What's a good Australian name, Amy?"

Wednesday at three o'clock in the Brier Hall cafeteria.
                    Signed,
                    Mathilda ("Matty") Owens

Within four days, "Matty" had her answer:

Dear Miss Owens,
I would definitely be interested in being interviewed by you—and so would a couple of my friends. Since you wanted more opinions about co-ed education, I'll bring them along. We will all be waiting in the cafeteria as you suggested and are looking forward to talking to you about our country.

                    Sincerely,
                    Robert Williams

CHAPTER 12

———◦———

That Wednesday, Kate clutched a notepad under one arm and her purse under the other and took one last look at herself in the mirror over Lisa's bureau.

Palmer had done her hair up in a beautiful French braid, then sprayed it with enough hair spray to guarantee it would stay in place. She'd also loaned her a pair of huge dark glasses and a big floppy felt hat that hid most of her face. Then, just to be safe, Kate borrowed a long, loose raincoat from Shanon and high boots from Lisa. By the time she was fully dressed, there was hardly an inch of Kate to be seen.

"Now there's absolutely *no* chance our pen pals will recognize you," Lisa said with satisfaction. "The boys only saw you once, anyway. And that was at the Halloween mixer, when you were wearing a costume that hid your face completely."

But even though Kate was again in disguise, Palmer had chosen and applied her makeup, which was just enough to highlight her best features—her eyes and high cheekbones.

With her hair and makeup done just right and wearing her best dress under Shanon's coat, Kate felt like a different person. A prettier person. Maybe even someone Reggie would like better than his new pen pal, Cindy.

Unfortunately, she wasn't sure what she would say or do if she *did* run into Reggie, now that she was supposed to be Mathilda Owens, not Kate Majors. She continued to worry about it as she bicycled slowly off to Brier Hall.

As previously arranged, Rob, John, and Mars were waiting for her in the cafeteria. Taking a moment to steady her jangled nerves, Kate concentrated on breathing evenly and unclenching her fists. Then she marched across the room.

"Hello, mates," she said brightly when she reached their table.

The three boys looked up curiously. Kate prayed that the accent and slang she'd practiced with Amy were good enough to fool them.

"Good afternoon," Rob said pleasantly. "Do you want something to drink? They have soda, cocoa, juice, and milk."

"They also have hot tea," John offered politely. "You Aussies drink a lot of tea, don't you?"

"Uh, yeah, I guess," Kate stammered, suddenly unsure of herself. "N-no thank you. I'm not thirsty." Actually her mouth was quite dry.

Rob shrugged and nodded toward an empty chair. "So what do you want to ask us?"

"Well," Kate cleared her throat, "I just have a few questions actually."

"That's all right. Ask as many as you want," Mars said

76

grandly. "It's quite an honor being interviewed for your school paper. Just think," he said, turning to John, "our words will be read by students halfway across the world."

"Hard to believe," John said, looking extremely pleased at the thought.

Kate glanced around the deserted cafeteria, even more nervous now that she was here. Although she hoped she might run into Reggie on her way back to her bike, which was locked up in the lot behind the building, she definitely didn't want him to appear and blow her cover while she was with The Unknown.

Kate touched the brim of the big hat to make sure it was securely in place and took a deep breath. "Well . . ." she began again. "For instance, do you eat your meals with the girls here at Brier Hall?"

"Yeah, we all eat at the same time," John said.

"And is the . . . uh . . . food good?" Kate asked, writing their answers on her pad.

Mars and Rob exchanged looks. "It's okay," Rob said.

"What about the social life?" Kate asked.

"Oh, that's interesting and very different from when we were at Ardsley," Rob answered without any hesitation.

"It's a lot more formal here," Mars put in. "They serve tea every afternoon, and have special dinners that everyone's supposed to dress up for."

"I see." Kate was scribbling madly.

The boys seemed to have no big complaints about Brier Hall, Kate thought, but the Foxes would be happy to hear that they weren't exactly raving about it either.

She glanced at the next question on her list. The girls had

spent a long time discussing exactly what she should ask.

"Are there dances or parties at Brier Hall that both the boys and girls go to?"

"So far, we've only—" Rob started to answer, but then his glance focused on a point beyond Kate's shoulder and he stopped in mid-sentence.

"Excuse me," he said quickly. "I'll be right back. There's someone I have to speak to."

Kate turned around to look at the doorway behind her, but a group of girls blocked her view.

"Sure," she said, "I'll just continue with your friends until you get back."

For a brief moment Kate wondered who Rob was talking to, but she was too busy questioning the other boys to worry much about it.

Rob returned to the cafeteria while Mars was telling Kate about the science labs at Brier.

"Excuse us for a moment," Rob said to Kate in a serious voice. He signaled to John and Mars, who huddled with him just beyond her hearing. Kate was beginning to get nervous again. What was going on?

A moment later the boys sat back down at the table. There was a long silence while they all stared at Kate. Then Rob said, "All right, Miss Owens, what else can we tell you?"

"Nothing really," Kate said, looking suspiciously at Rob. "I think I have just about all the information I need."

"Oh, but we want to make sure you understand how we feel about Brier Hall—this dream school."

"Dream school?" Kate's mouth dropped open.

"Yeah. It's too bad the exchange is only for a month. I

78

wouldn't mind staying here the rest of the school year," Mars said with obvious enthusiasm.

Kate opened up her notebook again and began writing.

"Everything here is really first-rate," John added. "Especially the girls. They're so much more sophisticated than the ones at the other schools around here—like at Alma Stephens."

Kate's head shot up and she glared at John, ready to argue the point. But just in time, she remembered who she was supposed to be. "Oh, do you really think so?" she asked mildly.

"*I* do," Rob said. "You should see this incredible foursome of girls who go to school here. They call themselves the Sisters, and they are *so* fantastic!"

"Really gorgeous," Mars said, pretending to fall over in a faint. "And they invite us to every tea and every dance," he said, sitting up straight again. "We usually sit with them at study hall and mealtimes."

Rob nodded solemnly. "Of course, they're great dancers, too."

"Really?" Kate was scribbling so fast she wasn't sure she'd be able to read her own writing later on.

"It sure is a great improvement over the old days," Rob said, grinning. "With any luck, they'll make this co-ed program permanent and we'll *never* have to leave!"

Kate snapped her notebook closed and stood up shakily. "That's enough," she choked out. "I mean . . . I think you've given me enough material for my article."

"Good," John said. "Will you send us a copy after it's published?"

"Oh, sure," Kate promised hastily as she grabbed her jacket and hurried out of the cafeteria.

Kate ran out the rear door of the building and started down the cement path toward her bike. She thought she heard someone laughing, and turned once to look behind her. But there was no one there, only a few big old trees, their leaves whispering softly in the cool spring breeze.

Poor Lisa, Shanon, and Amy, Kate thought. She was going to have to break the news to them very gently. They had definitely lost their pen pals!

CHAPTER 13

———◆———

Lisa, Amy, and Shanon listened in stunned silence while Kate read her notes out loud.

"Rob said *that?*" Lisa asked in amazement.

"What a bummer," Amy groaned, "especially after getting that letter."

"What letter?" Kate asked sympathetically. "Did one of your pen pals write to you?"

"Not a one," sighed Palmer, coming out of the bedroom. Even though Palmer had told Sam to stop writing to her, it was obvious to everyone that she missed his letters.

Lisa crossed to the desk. "We haven't heard a word from the boys," she told Kate grimly. "But Shanon picked this up at the *Ledger* office. It's from the Sisters."

"You mean they answered you?" Kate asked, wide-eyed.

Lisa held out a piece of pale yellow stationery with black curlicued handwriting:

Dear Foxes of the Third Dimension,
We think you have some nerve trying to grab credit for

81

*our idea of advertising at Ardsley for boy pen pals. And
where do you come off accusing us of stealing it from you?!
Even if you thought of the idea last fall, you must have
gotten it from us, because even though we didn't do anything about it then, we were already thinking about it. All
we can say is that you girls must be desperate for attention
if you'd stoop to trying to horn in on our publicity. You
sound very conceited in your letter, but we bet you're real
dweebs. And if we do get interviewed by another newspaper, you can be sure we'll tell them the truth—that we
thought of this original idea ourselves!*

Yours truly,
The Sisters

"What a mean letter," Kate said, wrinkling her nose.

"It's rotten," agreed Shanon. "Those girls don't sound
very nice."

"Maybe they didn't get their idea from us," said Amy,
"but they still didn't have to call us dweebs."

"*Desperate* dweebs!" Palmer pointed out, fluffing her
hair out in front of the mirror.

"We can't take this lying down," said Lisa. "I can't
believe Rob and John and Mars think they're so wonder-
ful."

Shanon shook her head. "I don't see how Mars could like
someone so . . . so . . ."

"So *conceited?*" Lisa said.

"That's what they said *we* were," Amy cried.

"I know," said Lisa, "but actually that's what they are.
Paige McGraw thinks she and the Sisters are going to get

famous just because they were written up in the Brighton *News*."

"They probably think they're going to get written up by *The New York Times* next," giggled Kate.

"I bet they're just waiting for some Hollywood producer to discover them," Amy piped up.

Shanon laughed. "And they called *us* conceited."

Lisa started laughing, too. But suddenly she stopped. "Wait a minute! I've got an idea!" she cried.

"How to get even with the Sisters?" Amy asked eagerly. "Tell!"

"What is it?" Shanon said. "Some kind of trick?"

"Maybe you should sneak over to Brier Hall and tie their sheets," Kate suggested conspiratorially. "Or Lisa could draw a weird-looking cartoon of them and we could run it in *The Ledger*."

"No, I have an even better idea," Lisa said excitedly. "Of course, you'd have to be pretty conceited to fall for it . . . But I bet it would work on them."

"What is it?" said Palmer, turning away from the mirror and giving Lisa her full attention.

Lisa pulled up a chair and grinned. "What would you do if a really famous group like New Kids on the Block asked us to be in a rock video?"

"I'd die!" screamed Amy. "It would be incredible."

"It would be amazing all right," agreed Shanon.

"What are you getting at, Lisa?" Palmer asked impatiently.

"Suppose New Kids on the Block wanted the Sisters in their new video? Just for a short appearance? Suppose the president of the New Kids' fan club had seen the Sisters' picture in the newspaper and wrote them about being in the video?"

"They're not the type," Amy said angrily. "*We* should be in the video. How come those snobs get to have the fun?"

"They're nothing but publicity hogs," complained Palmer.

Lisa laughed. "You don't understand. It didn't really happen. I just said *suppose* . . ."

"You're right," said Shanon. "I don't understand."

Lisa moved in closer. "Listen, suppose we wrote to the Sisters and made up a story like that. We could tell them to meet the fan club president someplace down in Brighton— like Figaro's."

"What good would that do?" Shanon asked, still bewildered.

Lisa shrugged. "If it was only a made-up story, then they would do nothing but sit there all day. The president wouldn't show up, and Paige and her friends would have wasted their whole afternoon."

"Not only that," Amy added, "they'd feel really dumb."

Palmer laughed. "I think it's a good trick. Then we'd just see who's conceited."

"You're not going to do it?" Shanon asked in a shocked voice.

"What harm could it do?" protested Lisa.

"And won't it be fun to sit there and watch them waiting hour after hour for the president of the fan club because they think they're going to be in a rock video?" Amy said with a chuckle.

"Wait a minute," said Shanon. "We're not going to Figaro's *ourselves*, are we?"

"Why not?" Lisa said, laughing nervously. "I hadn't actually thought of doing that, but now that you bring it up . . ."

Amy hastily grabbed a piece of stationery, making certain that it didn't match the blue paper they'd used for their first letter to the Sisters. "How's this?" she asked, scribbling quickly.

Shanon scanned Amy's note, gasping at the last paragraph:

So if you girls would be interested in appearing in New Kids on the Block's new video, please meet me at Figaro's Pizza in Brighton this Saturday at noon to discuss the details. A photographer will be there, so be sure to dress appropriately for publicity shots.

> *Sincerely,*
> *Paula Clark, President*
> *New Kids on the Block Fan Club*

"Who's this Paula Clark?" Shanon asked.

"It's a made-up name," explained Amy. "She doesn't exist."

"This sounds like something that might backfire," Kate warned them. "Maybe you should just write the letter but leave out the part about going to Figaro's."

"No way," Lisa chuckled. "I want to see the look on the Sisters' faces when no one shows up."

"Don't you think it's kind of mean?" Shanon said timidly.

"*I* think it's funny," said Amy. "Anyway, after the mean letter they wrote us, they deserve it."

"Let's do it!" cried Palmer.

"I hope we don't get caught," Shanon said, still doubtful. "Then we'll be the ones who are embarrassed."

"How could that happen?" Lisa said. "We'll just be sitting there eating our pizza."

Amy grinned. "And watching those conceited Sisters!"

"Count me out," Kate said firmly.

"Sure. This only involves the Foxes of the Third Dimension, anyway," said Lisa agreeably. "How about you Palmer?"

"What do you think?" Palmer said, her blue eyes flashing. "Just because my pen pal isn't involved in all this, that still doesn't mean those girls can call *me* a dweeb. Count me in, Foxes!"

CHAPTER 14

On the arranged day, the four Foxes managed to get passes to go into town to Figaro's. They hoped the Sisters had also been able to arrange for permission. Lisa, Shanon, Amy, and Palmer timed their arrival at the pizza place for ten minutes after noon, so they'd get there after the Sisters had arrived.

They strolled casually up to the wide plate glass window and pretended to read the menu that was taped up inside.

"I don't see them," Amy said as she peered into the restaurant's dark interior.

"Let me look," said Palmer, crowding up beside her. "There they are," she hissed. "In that corner toward the back."

"Oh my gosh," said Shanon. "Look at the way they're dressed!"

"You'd think they were all a bunch of debutantes, off to a Junior League meeting," Palmer murmured in disbelief.

It was true. The Sisters were geared out in pastel-colored cashmere sweaters over calf-length straight skirts. Two of the girls had on navy blue blazers, and the other two wore light blue jackets. They were all wearing high-heeled shoes, sheer stockings—and pearl jewelry!

"Those Brier girls are so conceited," Amy said. "They've actually bought our story!"

"Do you really think they have?" Shanon asked. "I mean, they'd have to be pretty dumb to fall for something like this."

"Well, they're here, aren't they?" Palmer sniffed. "So that just proves how dumb they are!"

"Now what?" Shanon asked uneasily. Although she wanted to teach these girls a lesson as badly as the rest of her suitemates, she wasn't sure this was really the right way. She suddenly wished she'd tried to talk Lisa out of her plan. She shot a worried look at Amy and Palmer, but they were looking at Lisa.

"We go in and order a pizza," Lisa said blithely. "Then we just wait and see what they do when no one shows up to meet them!" She let out a squeaky laugh, and before she could stop herself, Shanon was laughing, too.

The girls pushed through the door to Figaro's, with Lisa in the lead. They sat down near the front window. Two couples of college-age students and a family with a little boy in a high chair had already been served their pizza.

"Well, what should we have?" Lisa asked loudly enough to be heard by the Sisters on the other side of the little room.

"Let's get one large Monstro pizza—with everything on it," Shanon suggested.

"Fine with me," Amy said, casting a sideways glance at the Brier Hall girls.

"Me, too," Palmer added, "but forget the anchovies."

Lisa went up to the counter and placed their order, bringing back a pitcher of root beer with four glasses of ice on a tray.

"We can have some soda while we wait," she said. "And there should be plenty to go with the pizza, too."

Lisa was aware that the Sisters were watching them, maybe even talking about them, but she couldn't hear what they were saying because the jukebox was playing. At last the song ended, and no one put in any more quarters.

One of the Brier Hall girls checked her watch.

"What time is it, Paige?" the girl sitting beside her asked.

"Almost twenty after twelve," Paige said with a frown. "I wonder why she's late."

"Oh, don't worry. People in the entertainment business are never on time. It's not chic."

At this point, Amy started giggling. Lisa shoved an elbow in her ribs.

"Ow!" she cried.

The girl named Paige turned and looked at them, whispered something to her friends, and then all four began to titter.

"Paige, should we order a pizza or something?" one of the Brier girls asked hesitantly.

"Are you kidding, Patricia? That greasy stuff? Do you want to ruin your complexion?"

"The New Kids wouldn't want us in their video if we had zits all over our faces," the one called Brooke said solemnly.

This time Palmer clapped a hand to her mouth and bent over in a spasm of uncontrolled laughter. Then Amy started giggling again. Even Shanon cracked a shaky smile. Only Lisa was able to keep a straight face. She knew she had to do something quickly, or the whole plan would be ruined.

Impulsively, Lisa stood up and turned toward the Sisters' table.

"What are you doing?" Palmer managed between giggles.

"Just stay here and keep quiet," Lisa hissed between her teeth. She flashed Amy and Shanon a warning look, and the other two girls pulled themselves together.

Lisa squared her shoulders and strode across the room, taking a pencil and small notepad from her purse as she moved between tables.

When she was directly in front of the Brier girls, she stopped and asked, "Are you the girls from Brier Hall?"

They stared up at her.

"Yes," Paige said coolly. "Why?"

Lisa impulsively stuck out her right hand. "I'm Paula Clark, president of the New Kids on the Block Fan Club."

Behind her, Lisa heard a stifled gasp from the Foxes' table.

Paige flashed a wide smile showing off perfect white teeth. "So pleased to meet you," she said formally. "Please, *do* have a seat."

Lisa pulled a chair over from a nearby table.

"Where's the photographer?" one of the girls asked immediately, looking curiously around the room.

"Oh," Lisa ad-libbed, "he's coming a little later. I just wanted to explain a few things to you first—about the video, you know."

"Of course," said Paige. "We expected that. Go right ahead."

"Well, first of all, there's the fee you'll receive for appearing—"

"We get *paid* for being in the video!" Brooke gasped.

Paige gave her a withering glance, then turned quickly back to Lisa with an apologetic smile. "Of course we wouldn't accept any form of reimbursement."

"Well," Lisa said doubtfully, making a few marks on her pad, "I think there are union rules, or something like that."

Paige shrugged but couldn't help looking pleased. "Oh, well. If it's a rule, I guess we'll just have to take the money."

By now Palmer and Amy were helpless with laughter. Lisa turned around and caught Shanon cringing and glancing hopefully toward the door, obviously yearning to escape.

"*What* is wrong with those girls?" Paige asked, wrinkling her nose.

"They are so immature," another Sister commented huffily.

"Never mind them," Lisa said quickly. "Now, the question is, will you be able to get off from school for five days next month?"

"Get off from school? You mean, miss a whole week?"

"Possibly more," Lisa said seriously.

The Brier girls looked at each other, their smiles faltering.

"I don't know," one said. "Our headmistress is pretty strict. Can't they shoot the video on the weekend or something?"

They all looked so worried that Lisa nearly gave in to laughter herself. Then Paige's gaze swiveled around to take in the Foxes' table once more, and her expression changed.

"Hey, weren't you sitting over there with those strange girls a few minutes ago?"

Suddenly Lisa didn't feel like laughing anymore. She felt

her face turn warm with embarrassment as she realized she had no idea what to say next. "Excuse me for a minute," she finally managed. "I'll tell them to keep it down so we can talk."

She scooted back across the room to confer with her suitemates. "Keep it down," she warned them. "I think they're getting suspicious. Help me think . . . quick. What do I do now?"

"We'd better get out of here," Palmer said. "Go make some excuse for leaving."

"What should I say?" Lisa demanded. "Hurry, they're looking at us!"

"I don't know. Just *go*!" Palmer shooed her away.

Her face flaming, Lisa crossed the restaurant yet again. "I'm s-s-sorry," she stammered. "I'm afraid I have another appointment"—she glanced at her watch to give the proper effect—"in just fifteen minutes. More interviews for the video, you know. I'll, uh, I'll get back to you."

"But you don't even have our phone number!" one of the Brier girls objected.

"I don't believe she ever intended to get it," Paige said icily.

Then, just as Lisa was about to turn and run, Palmer and Amy came up beside her. She looked at Palmer, who shrugged her shoulders helplessly.

The trick clearly wasn't working out right. It was the Foxes, not the Sisters, who were feeling foolish.

Lisa stared down at her shoes, mortified. "Listen, I'm sorry," she mumbled. "This was supposed to be a joke, but I guess it's not very funny after all. We didn't mean to hurt your feelings or anything."

"What are you talking about?" Paige demanded, her eyes narrowing.

"I'm not the president of anyone's fan club," Lisa confessed in a shaky voice. "And the New Kids aren't planning on using you in a video. We're just students from Alma Stephens."

For a moment the Brier girls just stared at Lisa. Then Paige's mouth curled up haughtily. "You think we really believed any of that stupid story? Ha! We just came in here to have a pizza!"

One of the other Sisters moved over closer to Paige and tilted her nose at the identical angle to match her look of disdain. "Right. We always come here for lunch on Saturdays. Anyway, it's just like some silly Alma girls to play a stupid trick like this."

The Foxes stood there frozen, too embarrassed to respond.

"Come on," Paige said with a sniff. "We have more important things to do than hang out with these *children* any longer."

And with that, she and her friends swept out through the door.

CHAPTER 15

The early afternoon sun was streaming through the sitting-room window when the four girls from 3-D burst through the door, laughing hysterically. They all crowded into Lisa and Shanon's room, and flung themselves down on the twin beds.

At last Lisa caught her breath and wiped tears from her eyes with the back of one hand. "Do you believe we actually went through with that trick?"

Still giggling, Amy shook her head at Lisa and said, "I don't believe *you* actually went that far. I mean, we never planned for you to pretend to be the fan-club president."

"It seemed like a good idea at the time," Lisa said with a sigh. "But I was totally embarrassed when the Sisters really fell for it."

"You think *you* were embarrassed?" Palmer commented, rolling her eyes toward the ceiling. "I wanted to crawl under the table."

"Me, too," Shanon echoed.

"And I wanted to run out of there so fast you wouldn't have seen my dust." Amy laughed again, burying her face in Shanon's fluffy pillow.

Lisa shrugged. "I guess we all should have run out—before I got so carried away!"

Palmer got up off the bed and walked toward the window, a thoughtful expression on her face. "You know, if we'd planned it a little more carefully, we might have actually pulled it off."

"It doesn't matter now," Lisa said with a satisfied smile. "At least we proved how conceited and snobby the Sisters really are. They can pretend they just went to Figaro's for pizza, but we all heard them cutting down the food for being greasy. I'm sure they had no intention of actually eating there."

"That's right," Amy agreed. "And what's even better is that *they* know *we* know they were lying. I think we did teach them a lesson."

The four girls grinned, enjoying their triumph. But slowly, Lisa's smile faded.

Amy noticed and patted her friend on the back. "Is something wrong?"

Tipping her head to one side, Lisa turned her mouth down into a woebegone frown. "Playing the trick didn't help us get our pen pals back," she reminded the other Foxes.

"True," said Palmer, "but it sure made you forget about losing them for a little while. Me, too," she added.

Shanon sighed. "I still miss Mars's letters."

"And I miss John's," Amy said.

Lisa had just been thinking the same thing about Rob.

"I wish I hadn't told Sam off," Palmer admitted. "He'll probably never speak to me again."

Everyone was silent for a long moment.

At last, Lisa spoke up again. But this time her voice was almost a whisper. "I've sort of been thinking. Maybe The Unknown had a right to be mad at us for trying to tell them what to do, and for spying on them."

Amy winced. "You think so?"

"Yes," Lisa said. "After all, they were just taking advantage of a special program at Brier Hall. Rob was right when he said that it was his decision to make. What he takes for classes is really none of my business."

"I know I'd be pretty ticked off at John if he tried to tell me what courses to take," Amy chimed in.

The others nodded in agreement.

"What about the fact that we caught them sitting with the Sisters at the concert?" Lisa asked.

"That still might have just been chance," Shanon pointed out. "We never actually proved anything. But no matter how it happened, I can't believe our pen pals would really like those girls better than they like us."

Lisa nodded. "I think you're right. We are pretty special."

"The Foxes of the Third Dimension!" Amy said, smiling proudly. She turned to Palmer. "What about Sam? Do you *really* think he's gone forever?"

Palmer swallowed hard. "I don't know. I guess he had a right to be mad at me, too—for telling him how to dress. I may have been just teasing, but he certainly took me seriously. I should have known it might hurt his feelings."

"I wish we all had our pen pals back," Lisa whispered sadly.

It was almost dinnertime when Shanon remembered that no one had picked up the suite's mail. She volunteered to go to Booth Hall and returned a few minutes later, breathless and smiling.

"I can't believe it!" she said. "I got a letter from Mars!"

Lisa and Amy leaped up from the pink loveseat. "Anything for us?" they shouted.

Shanon shook her head apologetically. "Sorry."

"What's all the noise about?" Palmer demanded, sticking her head out of her bedroom door.

"Shanon got a letter from Mars," Amy explained. Although she was disappointed not to have gotten one from John, she was happy for her friend.

"Read it out loud," Palmer ordered.

"Okay." Shanon sat down on the floor right where she was, and the other girls gathered around her.

Dear Shanon,

I miss your letters a lot, and I guess the best way to get more of them is to write one to you—to explain a few things. First of all, yes, I was mad at you for spying on me. But I figure we're probably even now, because I did something to you that wasn't very nice either.

One day this girl reporter came to Brier Hall to interview The Unknown. Well, Rob, John, and I found out who she was (actually, Reggie showed up at the cafeteria and tipped us off that it was Kate Majors in disguise). Anyway, once we knew she was a friend of yours, we decided to play a trick on you girls. So we made up all sorts of crazy answers about

97

how we loved being at Brier and thought the girls here were
totally hot.

The more I think about it, the more I realize that was a
pretty mean thing to do, and I'd like to call a truce between
The Unknown and the Foxes. Rob and John don't agree
with me. I think they're still getting a thrill from their trick
and want to keep stringing your suitemates along. Mean-
while, would you start writing to me again? I'd really like
to hear from you.

Your lonely pen pal,
Mars

"Well, that explains that," Lisa said. "Mars is such a
decent guy, Shanon. You're really lucky."

"I know," Shanon said, planting a kiss on Mars's letter.
"He's so nice."

Dear Mars,

I miss your letters, too. All of us Foxes agree with you. No
more tricks. We want to call a truce, too. Please keep
working on Rob and John—maybe you can talk them into
writing to Lisa and Amy again.

Meanwhile, I'm so happy to be your pen pal again. I'll
write soon with all the latest news.

Your pal,
Shanon

"I have a feeling this is all going to work out fine," Amy
bubbled Monday morning as the girls started off to their
English class.

Lisa glared at her. "What are you talking about? Rob and John still aren't writing to us."

"I know," Amy said, "but we have the advantage now."

"Huh?"

"Don't you see?" she asked excitedly. "Now we know they still like us—that they were only conning us when Kate interviewed them."

The girls turned across the quad, toward Booth Hall.

"The question is," Lisa commented thoughtfully, "what are we going to do about it?"

Amy's dark eyes sparkled with mischief. Lisa stopped short and gave her suitemate a stern look. "Now hold on, Amy. Shanon just promised Mars that the Foxes wouldn't pull any more tricks."

"This isn't a trick," Amy objected. "We just need to give Rob and John a little encouragement, to convince them to start writing us again."

"And how do we do that?" demanded Lisa.

"Well . . ." Amy ran the tip of her tongue over her teeth. "I was just thinking that Visitor's Day is coming up this weekend. What if we planned a little face-to-face confrontation with our pen pals to clear the air?"

Lisa squinted at her suspiciously. "What sort of confrontation?"

"You'll see," Amy promised.

Dear Rob,

I'd like to invite you to Visitor's Day at Alma Stephens this Sunday. It starts at nine o'clock with a juice and donuts breakfast in Booth Hall. There will be special tours of the campus and a co-ed touch football game in the afternoon. If the weather is nice, we'll also have a cookout lunch with hamburgers and hotdogs.

I hope you'll like the idea and want to come, because I have something very important to say to you.

> *Yours truly, good weather or bad,*
> *Lisa*

Dear John,

Gee, it sure has been a long time since I heard from you. Guess you must be mammothly tied up with all your new classes at Brier Hall.

Well, I have a great solution. Why not come to Alma Stephens's Visitor's Day on Sunday. I'm sure you could use a break from all your hard work, or whatever has kept you from writing. Please come—there's something very important I want to tell you.

> *See ya,*
> *Amy*

"I hope this works," Amy said wistfully as she signed her note with a flourish.

Palmer nodded slowly. "I do, too. You know, I think I've changed my mind—I'm going to invite Sam, too. It's time we talked out our misunderstanding, face-to-face."

Dear Sam,

Alma Stephens is having a Visitor's Day open house this

Sunday. I'd appreciate it if you could come. If we're saying good-bye forever, I think it should be in person.

If you agree, I'll see you then.

Palmer

Dear Lisa,

I'm curious. What can you say to me on Visitor's Day that you couldn't write in your letter?

This seems very strange. I've talked it over with the other Unknowns and we've decided to come to Alma Stephens on Sunday, at least for a little while. There is so much neat stuff going on over here at Brier Hall that we hate to miss any of it. But, if what you have to say is really *important*, I guess I could spare a couple of hours.

Sincerely,
Rob

Dear Amy,

I'd really like to hear whatever it is you have to say. I only wish my schedule for the weekend wasn't so tight. I mean, there's a dance on Saturday and a special tea on Sunday— not to mention a couple of club meetings and the time I want to spend with a couple of new friends.

Oh, well, I guess it wouldn't hurt to take a rest from all this social stuff. I'll be there.

Hurriedly,
John

Lisa giggled as she and Amy switched letters. "Give me a break!"

"They really are laying this Brier Hall stuff on pretty thick," Amy agreed, grinning. She turned to face Palmer. "What does Sam's letter say?"

Palmer frowned slightly as she read:

Dear Palmer,
I'll be there,

Sam

Then she smiled. "I *knew* he'd come," she said smugly.

"What are you going to say to him?" Shanon asked curiously.

Palmer flashed her a mysterious look. "I think I've found the perfect way to convince Mr. Sam O'Leary that I don't judge people by the way they dress."

"For your sake, I hope it works," Shanon said, giving Palmer's hand a little squeeze.

"Oh," Palmer answered, looking not at all concerned, "I'd be willing to bet my best pearls that it will."

CHAPTER 16

The Foxes kept their fingers crossed all Saturday as the rain came down in gray sheets. More than anything in the world, they wanted the following morning to be clear so that Visitor's Day wouldn't be canceled.

Luckily, the downpour stopped sometime during the night. Early Sunday the sun appeared, drying off the stately old trees that lined the walkways across Alma's campus.

By eight-thirty when Lisa and Shanon went outside to test the thick green grass, it was still a little squishy underfoot. Otherwise the weather was beautiful.

The girls took a long time choosing their outfits for the day. Lisa wore turquoise jeans and a matching tie-dyed T-shirt. She chose a ruffled elastic band the same color as her jeans to pull her hair up in a ponytail.

Shanon braided her sandy-colored hair and tied it with a yellow ribbon, the same color as the flouncy yellow mini-skirt and matching cropped jersey she borrowed from Lisa.

Amy put on her best black jeans, rolled above the ankle,

and an oversized black T-shirt embossed with a gold tiger.

As usual, Palmer took the most care with her outfit. When she stepped out of the bedroom she and Amy shared, a full ten minutes after everyone else was dressed and waiting for her, the other girls just stared at her in amazement.

"Palmer? Didn't you, uh, forget something?" Amy asked when she finally found her voice.

"Forget something?" Palmer echoed, nonchalantly gazing down at the front of her sparkling white silk blouse and pretty pastel flowered skirt.

"Your shoes!" Lisa hooted. "Oh, Palmer, those are definitely not you."

They all stared at the pair of brown, unlaced hiking shoes on Palmer's narrow feet.

But Palmer was already heading for the door. "Oh, those," she said over her shoulder. "I just felt like a change." Then she turned around and grinned mischievously. "Think Sam will like them?"

"If you're trying to make him feel at home here at Alma, it should definitely work," Lisa commented.

"Good!" Palmer chirped. "Now let's go. We don't want to keep our pen pals waiting."

The girls walked together, along with flocks of other Alma students and a steady stream of guests arriving from the parking lot behind Booth Hall.

Inside the lounge, a long table had been arranged with trays of assorted donuts—jelly-filled, coconut-topped, sugar-glazed, chocolate-dipped—and crispy crullers. A second table held a coffee urn, silver tea service, and several pitchers of fresh orange juice.

"I don't see any of the boys yet," Shanon said.

"They'll show," Amy said with conviction. "They're too curious not to come."

Sure enough, a few minutes later Palmer spotted Sam O'Leary. She smiled broadly as he began picking his way through the crowd, but when he was only a few yards away, her jaw dropped.

"Oh, my!" she gasped. "Look what he's wearing!"

"I thought you weren't interested in clothes anymore," Lisa said impatiently.

"It's not th-that!" Palmer choked out, half laughing. "Just *look* at him!"

The Foxes turned and followed the direction of Palmer's astonished gaze. And there stood Sam, perfectly dressed in a navy blue blazer, white dress shirt, red-and-blue striped tie, and neatly laced black leather shoes.

Palmer stared down in dismay at her grubby hiking shoes. By the time she looked up, Sam had stopped in front of her.

"Hi," he said, his eyes following hers down to the floor.

For once in her life, Palmer found herself unsure of the proper thing to do in a social situation. "Hi," she said bleakly.

"Nice, uh, shoes," he commented with a straight face. Palmer raised her blue eyes to his gray ones, not sure whether he was teasing her.

"Well—" He bit his lip to keep from laughing, but Palmer caught the twinkle in his eyes. "They do look very practical," he went on. "I guess the ground is still a little muddy after all that rain."

"Yes," she agreed. "They definitely keep my feet dry."

Lisa nudged Shanon, who quickly grabbed Amy by the arm. The three girls moved away to give Palmer and Sam a chance to talk in private.

"I like your jacket and tie and all," Palmer said awkwardly. "But you didn't have to dress up just to please me. I told you clothes don't mean that much to me."

Sam laughed out loud then, but it was a pleasant laugh. "Palmer, clothes mean *everything* to you. You *love* clothes!"

She grinned at him sheepishly. "You're right. I do. But that doesn't mean I won't like you if you don't dress the way I do."

"I know that now. It must have taken a lot of nerve to show up in those hiking shoes."

She shrugged, but he was right. Now that he mentioned it, she felt as if everyone in the room was staring at her feet.

"And," Sam continued, "you don't have to dress to please me either. Let's just try to be ourselves. Okay?"

Palmer grinned at him. "Okay. We'll just dress the way we feel."

"Today I feel preppie," Sam said.

"And today *I* feel . . ." Palmer hesitated, giggling at herself, ". . . like I always feel. These shoes are *horrible!*"

Sam chuckled with her. "They *are* pretty tacky-looking with such a pretty skirt and blouse. I'll walk you back to Fox Hall and you can change into something more comfortable—or should I say *less* comfortable!"

"Thanks," she said gratefully as Sam took her hand, and together they walked out of the lounge.

Meanwhile, Lisa, Amy, and Shanon were still searching for their pen pals among the growing crowd.

"Oooh, there's Mars!" Shanon cried suddenly.

"And John and Rob are right behind him," Amy said, her eyes growing wide. "Ready, Lisa?"

"Ready."

The three girls crossed the room toward the donut table where the boys were already helping themselves. Mars held half a chocolate-glazed donut in his fingers. John and Rob were busy pouring orange juice.

"Glad you could come," Lisa said with a smile for Rob.

He grinned, then switched expressions to give her a cool look. "Hi," he returned, picking up a jelly donut.

Shanon and Mars looked at each other and smiled conspiratorially. It was obvious to them that Rob was really happy to see his pen pal.

"Come here," Mars said, grabbing Shanon's hand. "I have something to show you." They quickly disappeared into the crowd.

"I hope Mars isn't planning on going very far," John commented seriously. "He knows we can't stay long."

Rob nodded, then looked at Lisa. "Our social schedule is so tight these days. Teas and dances every single day almost. It's totally exhausting. So—what did you girls want to tell us?"

Lisa flashed Amy a mischievous look. "Well," she said, stifling a smile, "we know how much you like the girls at Brier Hall."

"They *are* pretty cool," Rob agreed.

Lisa nodded. "That's what we figured. So Amy and I thought we'd let you off the hook."

"The hook?" Rob and John asked, clearly puzzled.

"Since you found girls you like better than us," Amy

explained, sounding very logical, "you'll probably want to write to them once you go back to Ardsley."

"You won't have time to write to us and to them, too," Lisa added, "so it only makes sense that the Foxes and The Unknown stop being pen pals."

Rob stared at John in shock, then snapped around to face Lisa. "Is . . . is this for real?"

"Of course," Lisa said calmly. "We wouldn't want pen pals who don't want us. That wouldn't be fair." Even though she made her voice sound strong, Lisa was shaking inside. What if Rob actually agreed that they shouldn't write anymore? That would be awful.

"Gee, Amy," John stammered. "I don't know . . ." He hesitated, looking at Rob for help.

"What he's trying to say," Rob said firmly, "is that we don't really like the girls at Brier Hall all that much."

"In fact, we *hate* going to Brier Hall and can't wait to get back to Ardsley," John admitted all in a rush. "The food is terrible—"

"They make us dress up and go to tea every day," Rob interrupted.

"And the girls are unbelievably snobby," said John, shaking his head. "We were just teasing you girls about the dances. There hasn't been a single one. And even if there was, I'm not sure I'd want to go to it."

Lisa and Amy couldn't restrain themselves any longer. They broke out in laughter. "We know! We know!"

Confused once more, Rob and John stared at each other.

"We can't tell you where we got our information, but we heard you were playing a trick on us," Lisa explained.

"We're not mad though," Amy said quickly. "We just

want to be friends again. We really missed getting your letters."

"We did, too," Rob said happily. "In fact, we were trying to figure out how to end this joke and get things back to the way they were before."

Just then Mars and Shanon returned, still holding hands.

"Look what Mars gave me!" Shanon cried enthusiastically. She pointed to a metal button on her jersey. It read:

I AM A SOCIAL ANIMAL!

"Oh, wow!" Amy said. "I love it!"

"I had them made to order," Mars announced proudly. He stuck another button just like it on his own shirt front, then dug into his pocket and pulled out a whole handful of the small round disks.

"Fantastic!" Lisa cried. "Now we can *all* be social animals. Wait till Palmer sees these!"

"I have another present for you girls," Mars said, dramatically pulling a plastic bag out of his jacket pocket like a magician pulling a bunny from a hat.

Lisa stared at the bag. "Looks like a bunch of stale old rolls."

"Exactly," said Mars. "Stale rolls from the Brier Hall dining room."

"Not only were they snobby and formal there," John explained, "but the food was disgusting."

"Well, I've found a use for them," Mars claimed. "After the co-ed football game this afternoon, I'm using these rolls in a very special test."

"Not another one of your quizzes!" Rob groaned good-naturedly.

"It's a very easy and harmless test," Mars objected. "I'll

109

even let you take it right now, if you like. There are just two choices: given the opportunity to either eat one of these rolls or throw it—which would you do?"

"*Throw it!*" Rob shouted, grabbing a roll out of the bag and heaving it at John.

John laughed, seized another roll, and chased Rob outside onto the grass. "After the last three weeks at Brier," he shrieked, "I *need* a good food fight!"

With peals of laughter, the girls joined in, grabbing rolls and following the boys outside.

They were holding the bread ready to fire when a stern voice commanded, "Stop that this instant!"

They all spun around, and Lisa was sure they'd been caught red-handed by the headmistress, Miss Pryn, who would take a dim view of such uninhibited behavior on Visitor's Day. But instead they found themselves face-to-face with Kate Majors.

Kate stood in front of them, her fists propped on her hips, a look of disapproval on her face. She was wearing her glasses again, but she had on a little makeup and a dusty rose sweater that must have been new. She looked much softer and prettier than usual, Lisa thought approvingly.

However, Kate was clearly furious. "This is totally against the rules!" she scolded.

"But we were just—" Shanon began.

"I should report you to Miss Pryn this very minute," Kate threatened. "She will be very upset with—"

Suddenly Kate stopped short, her eyes fixed on a spot just behind Lisa.

Lisa spun around to see her brother, standing like a statue, speechless.

"Uh, hello . . . everyone," Reggie stammered uneasily.

Kate hesitated with her mouth open, as if deciding whether to smile at Reggie or keep on yelling at the others.

Finally, Lisa took over. "Hi, Reggie," she said smoothly. "Glad you could come to Visitor's Day. Doesn't Kate look great today?"

Reggie blushed, then looked Kate over self-consciously. "You look really nice, Kate. Did you do something different with your hair?"

"Yes," she mumbled, her face flushing with pleasure.

"You should wear it that way all the time," Reggie said, smiling more easily now. And then, in a low voice that only Kate could hear, he added, "I always knew you were pretty smart, but today you look pretty *and* smart!"

CHAPTER 17

Dear Kate,

I'm glad I got a chance to see you on Sunday for Visitor's Day at Alma. I have a confession to make. I kind of started writing to a girl at Brier Hall last month, and that's why I stopped writing to you. But she wasn't very smart. She didn't even know what Star Wars meant when I wrote to her about the President's defense plans. (She thought I meant the movie!)

Anyway, I'd really like to start writing to you again. I hope you'll answer this letter.

By the way, I sort of saw you the day you were at Brier, interviewing Rob and his roommates. I noticed that you weren't wearing your glasses. I hope it's not because you're self-conscious about wearing them. I like girls with glasses. I think they look very intelligent.

Sincerely,
Reggie

Dear Reggie,

It's a good thing you like me in glasses, because contacts were a disaster with a capital D! And, yes, I'd definitely like to start writing to you again. I think we have a lot in common.

Yours truly,
Kate

P.S. I think you're very intelligent, too.

Dear Mars,

Thanks to you, I've become a truly Social Animal. I've worn your button every day to class this week. And do you know what? People who never spoke to me before—even some fifth-formers—have come up to ask me what it means. I've made a lot of new friends that way.

They all want to know where I got my button. They want one, too.

I know you're always looking for ways to earn extra money. How about going into the button business?

Socially yours,
Shanon

Dear Shanon,

Hey! That's cool about people being interested in my buttons. Maybe I will consider going into mass production! It might be a good way to save up money for college.

Seriously, though, the Social Animal stuff is just for fun. I wouldn't dream of trying to put you in one particular category. You're Shanon Davis . . . just yourself. That's what's so cool about you and why I like you so much. There is definitely no one quite like you.

> An Animal Like No Other,
> Mars

Dear Rob,

I'm sorry we didn't get much time to talk in private at Visitor's Day. I just want to apologize for all the mean things I said about Brier Hall. I guess I was just jealous. I also shouldn't have sent Kate to "interview" you. I don't blame you for being mad at me, but I hope you aren't anymore—mad at me, I mean.

> Your pen pal, still,
> Lisa

Dear Lisa,

Well, since you're apologizing, I guess I should too. Making up crazy answers to give Kate when she was interviewing us wasn't nice at all. I guess I never thought you'd take it seriously. Then, when you did, I was too embarrassed to tell you the truth.

When you think about it, though, none of the tricks really changed anything. I'm just glad that we're both writing again.

> Your pen pal,
> Rob

P.S. Just for the record—I'm not mad anymore.

Dear John,

There's one question I never had a chance to ask you on Sunday: What exactly does your "Farewell" poem mean?

I'm really curious. Because I thought I knew, but now I'm not sure.

Please write your answer soon.

Best wishes,
Amy

Dear Amy,

You asked about my Farewell poem? Well, it's sort of strange, but at the time I wrote it, it didn't really mean anything. I just thought it was dramatic. I'm certainly not going anywhere.

However, I finished another poem this morning. Pay close attention to the acrostic in this one. It has a special message just for you:

> *In the thick of it now*
> *Living free at last*
> *Invisible fingers make prints on glass*
> *Kites flip in the breeze*
> *Everybody is pleased*
> *You're the best though*
> *Oh, A.H.*
> *United we stand.*

Do you like it? I hope so.

Your poetic pen pal,
John

"I-L-I-K-E-Y-O-U," Shanon spelled out with a long, dreamy sigh. "Oh, that's so romantic."

"It is, isn't it?!" Amy said, grinning proudly. "I think I'll write a new song and ask John to make up the lyrics."

"I think you should forget about rock and write a musical," Palmer said. "I love Broadway shows!"

Amy giggled. "We'll write one just for you, Palmer. About a beautiful young blonde who stars in a show and falls in love with the handsome leading man."

Lisa turned to Palmer. "Speaking of leading men, did you write to Sam?"

"Of course," Palmer exclaimed.

Dear Sam,

I'm glad we got to see each other on Sunday. And I'm also glad you're not still mad at me. I guess I was being just a little bit snobby about your friends. Being at a big noisy basketball game is just not my thing. At least, it hasn't been in the past. And I really felt out of it, being so overdressed for the basketball game. I've never actually been to one before. I hope you understand.

> *Sincerely,*
> *Palmer Durand*

Dear Palmer,

Yes, I understand. In fact, I was being a snob, too. I like dressing preppie, but I don't like being the same as everyone else, so I got upset when you called me a preppie—even though maybe I am, at times. In fact, when I changed schools from Ardsley to Brighton, it was a problem. I tried dressing the way I had at Ardsley (shirt, tie, dress pants), but the other students just wouldn't give me the time of day. It

116

wasn't until I started dressing like them that they made me feel welcome here.

Anyway, when all is said and done, what really counts about people is who they are, not how they look. A personality is what really counts. And you, Palmer, have a ton of personality. So do your suitemates, come to think of it! The Foxes can't be classified, by Mars or anyone else. You're all one of a kind, especially you, babe.

Love,
Your Number One Preppie,
Sam

Something to write home about . . .

another new Pen Pals story!

In Book Ten, Palmer has problems—lots of them! First her class adviser, Mr. Griffith, puts her on academic warning. Then her parents cut off her allowance. And as if that isn't bad enough, her pen pal Sam O'Leary stops writing to her. It's a good thing Palmer still has her friends. At least she can count on them. Or can she . . . ?

Here is a scene from Pen Pals #10: PALMER AT YOUR SERVICE.

Palmer glanced at the crumpled piece of scrap paper on which Shanon had scrawled her mother's recipe. The next step on the list was beating the batter. Palmer checked the cabinets for an electric mixer but couldn't find one. Instead, she grabbed a big wooden spoon. Though she'd never beaten a cake by hand herself, she'd seen her mother's cook in Florida do it.

Sticking the spoon into the first bowl, Palmer began whipping at the batter, but after only a minute or so her arm got tired. Beating a cake was hard work. She looked at the recipe. She wondered if there were any special instructions about beating by hand. Finding nothing like that on the front, she turned the paper over. But the only thing on the back was an old letter. It appeared to be something Shanon had written to Mars but never sent.

Palmer eagerly scanned Shanon's writing. A little voice inside told her she was being nosy, but another voice insisted Shanon wouldn't mind. After all, the girls in Suite 3-D shared practically all their pen pal correspondence, at least the letters *from* the boys. The short note was very matter-of-fact. It was Shanon's invitation to Mars for the fund-raising mixer. Palmer thought it was pretty dull until she came to the P.S.—"Palmer did not invite her mom and dad to Parents' Weekend. I think she's kind of weird."

"Weird!" Palmer breathed aloud. "What's that supposed to mean?" Her eyes smarted with angry tears. All this time she'd thought Shanon was her friend. But it was obvious she wasn't. Palmer read the letter over again, and then again. . . .

How could Shanon have been so disloyal? And how can Palmer ever forgive her?

P.S. Have you missed any Pen Pals? Catch up now!

PEN PALS #5: SAM THE SHAM

Palmer has a new pen pal. His name is Sam O'Leary, and he seems absolutely perfect! Palmer is walking on air. She can't think or talk about anything but Sam—even when she's supposed to be tutoring Gabby, a third-grader from town, as part of the school's community-service requirement. Palmer thinks it's a drag, until she realizes just how much she means to little Gabby. And just in time, too—she needs something to distract her from her own problems when it appears that there *is* no Sam O'Leary at Ardsley. But if that's the truth—who *has* been writing to Palmer?

PEN PALS #6: AMY'S SONG

The Alma Stephens School is buzzing with excitement—the girls are going to London! Amy is most excited of all. She and her pen pal John have written a song together, and one of the Ardsley boys has arranged for her to sing it in a London club. It's the chance of a lifetime! But once in London, the girls are constantly supervised, and Amy can't see how she'll ever get away to the club. She and her suitemates plot and scheme to get out from under the watchful eye of their chaperone, but it's harder than they thought it would be. It looks as if Amy will never get her big break!

PEN PALS #7: HANDLE WITH CARE

Shanon is tired of standing in Lisa's shadow. She wants to be thought of as her own person. So she decides to run for Student Council representative—against Lisa! Lisa not only feels abandoned by her best friend, but by her pen pal, too. While the election seems to be bringing Shanon and Mars closer together, it's definitely driving Lisa and Rob apart. Lisa's sure she'll win the election. After all, she's always been a leader—shy Shanon's the follower. Or is she? Will the election spoil the girls' friendship? And will it mean the end of Rob and Lisa?

PEN PALS #8: SEALED WITH A KISS

When the Ardsley and Alma drama departments join forces to produce a rock musical, Lisa and Amy audition just for fun. Lisa lands a place in the chorus, but Amy gets a leading role. Lisa can't help feeling a little jealous, especially when her pen pal Rob also gets a leading role—opposite Amy. To make matters worse, the director wants Rob and Amy to kiss! Amy is so caught up in the play that she doesn't notice Lisa's jealousy—at first. And when she finally does notice, the damage has already been done! Is it too late to save their friendship?

WANTED: BOYS — AND GIRLS —
WHO CAN WRITE !

Join the Pen Pals Exchange and get a pen pal of your own!
Fill out the form below.
Send it with a self-addressed stamped envelope to:

PEN PALS EXCHANGE
c/o The Trumpet Club
PO Box 632
Holmes, PA 19043
U.S.A.

In a couple of weeks you'll receive the name and address
of someone who wants to be your pen pal.

ut here ---

PEN PALS EXCHANGE

NAME _____ GRADE _____

ADDRESS _____

TOWN _____ STATE _____ ZIP _____

DON'T FORGET TO INCLUDE A STAMPED ENVELOPE
WITH YOUR NAME AND ADDRESS ON IT!